*Obscurity*

THE
SEAGULL
LIBRARY OF
FRENCH
LITERATURE

# *Obscurity*

## PHILIPPE JACCOTTET

Translated by Tess Lewis

LONDON NEW YORK CALCUTTA

INSTITUT
FRANÇAIS
INDIA

Liberté • Égalité • Fraternité
RÉPUBLIQUE FRANÇAISE
AMBASSADE DE FRANCE EN INDE

This work is published with the support of
Institut français en Inde – Embassy of France in India

swiss arts council
**prohelvetia**

The first edition of this publication was supported by a grant
from Pro Helvetia, Swiss Arts Council

**Seagull Books**, 2022

Originally published in French as Philippe Jaccottet, *L'Obscurité*

© Editions Gallimard, Paris, 1961

First published in English translation by Seagull Books, 2015
English translation © Tess Lewis, 2015

ISBN   978 1 8030 9 055 9

**British Library Cataloguing-in-Publication Data**
A catalogue record for this book is available
from the British Library

Typeset in Fournier MT by Seagull Books, Calcutta, India
Printed and bound by WordWorth India, New Delhi, India

I

When I returned to our native country, several years had passed since I'd last seen my master—I called him this because under him I'd learnt the essentials of what guided me. It was he, in fact, who had imposed the separation—he feared, no doubt rightly, that I might confuse the two of us, that in following him too closely I would lose all sense of personal existence. Because I was on another continent and he had almost completely given up all involvement in public life—his retirement to the country allowed him, in a sense, to extinguish the splendour of his reputation—I'd heard nothing more about him. I didn't even know if he was still alive. His teachings, on the other hand, had borne fruit. I came back full of strength, no longer afraid of the worst. Even so, the memories of what I'd witnessed first-hand over the years—instances of injustice, of stupidity or brutality—were enough to cut the appetite for life even in men less sensitive than I. I hadn't distanced myself from the world in the slightest and could not find a word strong enough to describe its infamy. Yet had I witnessed even more, the energy with which I was armed would nonetheless have kept me standing, overcome at once with stupor and, as strange as it may seem, with joy, with a sense of expectancy no reasonable man would have understood. I'd had several affairs but I returned alone. And when I began searching for traces of my master from almost the very moment I disembarked, it was with the thought, one I barely admitted to myself, that his student had surpassed him, that he would be proud to see his teachings so fully assimilated, so intensely experienced. First, I wrote to the village where he was living with his family at the time I decided to leave and where I had spent such wonderful days in their company. When I received no answer, I assumed that he must have resolved, for the sake of his child's education, to do what he dreaded and moved back to the city. All the same, I was surprised to see 'Unknown' stamped on the envelope next to his name. Several mutual friends admitted they had completely lost sight of him; they'd obviously not forgiven him his retreat into regions of silence that had always been foreign to them. Since he was the one who had sought out obscurity, they were not about to go and retrieve him. My surprise only increased, and even took on shades of apprehension—I began to wonder if perhaps he, too, had left for distant lands as he had occasionally dreamt of doing. Finally, after two weeks in which my inquiries  grew increasingly anxious, I decided to seek out an old poet whom, I remembered in time, my master had admired without reservation for the grace that characterized even his most trivial writings. When I asked this poet if he knew what had become of the man who was one of his work's most devoted admirers, he gave such a deep sigh that I was afraid I would never see my master again, a fear I had not clearly admitted until that point. The poet then told me, once he remembered who I was and what ties had bound us, that my master had abandoned his wife and child more than a year earlier and that she had come to see him, greatly distressed, and had confided in him. She knew where her husband was hiding, almost completely destitute, in a miserable rented room in the large city where his glory had once shone so brightly. He refused to see her, both her and his son, although he had left them almost everything he owned. Nor had any of his friends crossed his doorstep. He himself, the old poet—whose eyes already seemed to have lost sight of this world and to be focused only on the narrow passage he would have to cross to leave it—was too weary even to try to see him. I asked the poet if he knew what could have driven my master to this, if the young woman had explained the tragedy. She'd merely maintained that her husband had been overcome with despair extremely abruptly as if stricken with an illness, that he'd refused to speak to her about it and that he disappeared not long after, 'like one of those dogs that doesn't want to be seen dying'. The only thing he asked of her was that she forget him, make herself a new life immediately and never concern herself with him again.

I took my leave distractedly, alarmed by the catastrophe so suddenly revealed to me. I did not hesitate long, however, over what to do next. I wrote to my master, now that I had his address, telling him I had returned and was eager to see him. He wrote the following day that he would be expecting me at his home at the end of the day.

On the way, my spirit unsettled as much by curiosity as worry, I couldn't help but reflect on the circumstances under which I first met the man I was now almost afraid to see again. The radiance of his intelligence was so great at the time that many sought him out as a mentor or companion. I was still very young then in that big city where all I saw around me was a chaos of passions and ideas both attractive and horrifying and, anxious not to lose myself in this chaos, I was convinced by everything I'd heard about him that he could help me. I'd wanted only to ask him to bring some order to the myriad temptations assailing me, and the possibilities opening before me. I was one of those prudent souls who need someone to chart them a course or soon believe themselves lost. I can at least recognize my own merit in having wanted that course to be the most just even if it was likely to be difficult.

I had learnt that a discreet official ceremony had been organized to sanctify the reputation of this man whom I knew solely by his renown. I didn't want to let my anticipation of the inevitable theatricality of such public events dissuade me—no, I wanted only to determine if this man truly had some secret, if the source of the splendour attached to his name was, in fact, in his own heart and not in something outside him, as is too often the case. At the very last minute, my dread of the throng, of not behaving properly, combined with an almost greedy sense of expectation, almost drained my resolve to enter the building in which I knew the soirée was being held. Nonetheless, there I was, a few minutes later, standing in the alcove of a high window, from which I could observe in turn the still lively street, the windows of the building opposite and the reception rooms filled with a chattering crowd. It seemed that no matter how long I lived I would never find my place in these gatherings, to which the participants come primarily to display themselves. Only when I noticed dusk was falling outside (it was early spring) did I realize the time had come for me to make a move if I did not want to have insinuated myself there in vain. Scanning one room and then another, my eye was caught by a large brown-and-black silk shawl framing the face of one of the few women at the soirée, probably the wife of the consul hosting the reception. Her face was rather pale and so noble, so ardent that it reminded me of the heroines in old novels. Beside her stood the man I so longed to meet. What immediately struck me about him was something I spontaneously translated to myself as *poverty*. His evening wear was perfectly correct, a white silk shirt and patent leather shoes; yet you could sense that each item must have been carefully chosen to feign supreme elegance without incurring the actual cost. Wealth is always marked by a certain ease, even insolence, which was entirely lacking in this man although you could not claim he was ill at ease. Still, what surprised me even more is that his features resembled those of a destitute man. In recounting that evening later, I'd have liked to have been able to say that while his apparel betrayed some effort made to ape worldly elegance, the splendour of his spirit, the radiance of his eyes—what do I know?—clearly showed what constitutes true wealth. But that was not remotely the case. Our hostess had very gentle dark eyes and that nobility of spirit I just mentioned. Near her stood a short, vigorous man in whom I thought I recognized a philosopher very much in fashion at the time. He was the only guest in a business suit—no doubt far above such niceties as dress—and he talked ceaselessly, in short phrases delivered rapidly and with emphatic gestures, as if he were too intelligent to linger on any subject for long and wanted to prove it. The guest of honour, however, went almost unnoticed, his features perhaps worn by a difficult existence or, rather, masked by a film of dust (like those beautiful objects in old residences or provincial museums that no one visits). And so that night for the first time I listened to him speak in a low voice but with a rather engaging tone that suggested he was listening to himself with one ear—out of circumspection, I decided, rather than complacency. His comments could just as well have been made by any other guest, if, that is, they themselves were not eccentric or at least were not trying to seem so. Maybe he knew some great truths, some hidden marvels (I would later convince myself he did), but no one would have believed it based on his conversation that night. Indeed, I noticed that he was trying to say only things that were just and true even if too severe or serious for the circumstances, but these words, too, were dulled by a kind of veil. And once I finally sat down in order to follow the conversation more closely, I noticed that he evaded certain questions, particularly those hurled at him by the short, jabbering philosopher, and chose his words carefully as obstacles to mask his retreat. As he retreated in this curious fashion, with a weary air, his eyes lingered on the hostess' hand as if examining the opal that adorned it and scrutinizing its milky gleam for the one answer that seemed worth giving.

The consul said a few words in the middle of the evening, after which most of the guests began to slip away. The guest of honour did not wait long to follow their lead, discreetly, as if afraid of attracting attention one last time. I decided to follow him, at that point much more fascinated by an obscure aspect of his character I thought I perceived than by his name.

As for me, I have resolved not to reveal anything more about myself than is necessary to avoid any ambiguity in this account. I will simply note, therefore, that I was a dozen or so years younger than the illustrious figure whose voice I heard for the first time that evening with an astonishment that verged on disappointment. I felt rather miserable and my desire to overcome this sense of misery was strong enough for me to trail the man I believed could become my guide. I didn't know at the time if I would ever approach him; naively I thought it might be enough for me to listen to him, to spy on him . . . If his illustriousness proved pure, I would no longer be adrift. (Those are indeed the thoughts of a young man!) All I really wanted was to walk in the same light, in the beauty of the light in which I believed he was immersed. Full of presumption, I dreamt of joining him; and on that March night shortly after the war, I began by following him along the dark narrow streets through which he walked rapidly, as if fleeing some danger, perhaps the danger represented by the clamorous world we'd just left behind.

I was amazed at one point to see him break into a run after checking his watch. Why was he late and if he did have a rendezvous, why had he scheduled it for that very evening? Why on earth didn't he just hail a cab? Whatever the reason, I had to quicken my pace to keep him in sight. Luckily, the street down which I chased him was one of those long straight streets that run parallel to the river, and are as quiet as the quays are clogged with cars. I could see his slender silhouette, which now seemed immeasurably small, made smaller still by his breathless haste at the foot of those tall, massive buildings that looked uninhabited. (He stopped frequently to catch his breath, once he even wiped his forehead with the back of his hand.) There wasn't much light. The courtyard trees that extended their branches over the walls here and there were black and it was only at the intersections, because of the corner cafes, that life and lights returned momentarily. I was briefly distracted by an argument taking place before one cafe and when I resumed my absurd shadowing down a street about to end in a high transverse wall behind which gardens lay, I could no longer find the man I was pursuing. I retraced my steps, jostled by bystanders drawn to the escalating argument. I looked down the cross street dotted with illuminated terraces that led to the river and spied him in front of one of these terraces, leaning forward, supporting himself with his hand on the back of a wicker chair. A few seconds later, he straightened and entered the room somewhat brusquely, without looking to the left or right, like someone trying to master a deep fright. I had enough time to realize that, carried away by his slightly mad dash, he was surely focused only on the end of his race; he hadn't wasted a glance at any passer-by or car. Since he didn't know me, I could safely sit near him without attracting his attention.

A very young girl, whose elongated eyes in her round, pale face with Asian features I found striking, was waiting for him with a smile and the amused, slightly worried air of a child caught disobeying. He pushed aside a chair to shake her hand, then sat down facing her and initially seemed to be trying to catch his breath. Perhaps he was also shaking off the final memories of the evening. I was beginning to understand just how much of a burden it must have been for him.

I cannot express how deeply this scene touched me, banal as it was. If at first disappointed in him, I was delighted to discover in this man a hopeless and maybe unhappy lover. He felt so close to the young man I was at the time that I resolved then and there to approach him one day, either by writing to him or going to see him. I also wanted to keep spying on him, even if it was indiscreet. I got up when they did. I saw him offer her his arm and watched them head slowly towards the river. On the quay, I was separated from them for a moment by the stream of cars and could not find them again . . . Nevertheless, within a few weeks I had become one of his friends and, in a sense, his student—indeed, at no point in my studies had I listened to any teacher with such rapt attention and such happiness.

The memory of this pursuit, already distant, now gave me the idea that in not only fleeing a superficial society and his burdensome reputation but in breaking bonds infinitely more constricting and real, he had perhaps wanted once again, not without cruelty towards others this time, to run towards something precious, to escape a kind of death for some new beginning . . . But what kind of new beginning? What connection could there be between the sound and fury of fame and the quiet happiness I saw in him later? My supposition that he had fled towards another love seemed extravagant to me, although I wasn't sure why: What adventure more beautiful than his life was at the time could possibly have tempted him? In any case, despite my very real anxiety, I was still hesitant—I have to admit—to see his surprising decision as a defeat or a simple evasion because I was so used to considering him a man of accomplishment and success. Perhaps, I thought in an attempt to reassure myself, he has donned the garb of a desperate man in order to triumph all the more? Was it possible that I would find a sage divested of his most valuable possessions and illuminated by that dispossession?

All the same, I was no longer one to pursue him through the fine streets near the river (where, for that matter, he would surely not be able to run for long). I now followed the endless modern avenues that led to the southern half of the city, through neighbourhoods that became increasingly bleak and deserted the further I went. And so I ended up in the vicinity of an old train station that, although of minor importance, was significant enough to bring a bit of life and colour back to the square in front of it and the streets leading towards it. It was a neighbourhood of dubious nightclubs, shady cinemas and brasseries filled with derelicts from the beginning of the century. In the hotels surrounding the station, most of them hourly hotels, you heard the screeching of the trains, and flashes from the streetcars reflected in the mirrors adorned abject pleasures with furious fleeting crowns. I remembered having once walked these streets at the break of dawn, a ghost surprised by even the muddiest light, at the side of a woman who was like a stream of milk in the night, something soft and dangerously obscure, whose every dream, every gesture was boldness itself. I thought I'd completely forgotten her, so brief was her passage through my hesitant youth. Returning to this neighbourhood, which I'd avoided after our separation, suddenly brought her back to me intensely if not distinctly— rather like the uncertain source of muddled images and fragments of images, accompanied by a terribly bitter feeling in which I was forced to acknowledge some regret. When I finally stood before the building in which my master was waiting for me, my mind, surprisingly, was not preoccupied with him, with my many memories of him, but was distracted from thoughts of the present, of our imminent meeting. My mind was filled instead with those images and scraps of older images, deceptively sombre and tender, through which I saw us again passing from the golden warmth of the night into the morning's grey clamminess in an unfamiliar world, completely separate from the world in which others apparently continued to lead their lives, even though our path crossed theirs and we were continually being elbowed, jostled and eyed by them.

I paused for a moment in the dark, windowless corridor, both to regain my bearings and to shake off the dank insinuation of images so persuasive that if I had not pushed them aside, I would have had the feeling I was not entering my master's house alone. I no longer felt at all prepared to face this meeting from which I had no idea what to expect. For a brief moment, I was tempted to turn around. Looking back now at my hesitation in the building's dilapidated labyrinth, I believe that, almost unconsciously and for an instant, I associated the extreme tenderness I felt when the images inundated me at the sight of the train station with my avid curiosity about where my master's recent flight had led him or was meant to lead him—as if he had intended to find refuge in a place favourable to such images; as if he were going to help me, yet again, to live, to expunge all sense of loss and all regret. Yes, it must have been that thought, replete with an almost sensual curiosity, full of milk and darkness, that sudden, greedy, audacious thought that decided me.

The concierge mentioned the far end of a hallway with the aggressive curtness of those who save their eloquence for the useless or false, neglecting to tell me that there were no fewer than three doors at the hallway's end. There was no answer to my first knock. Two of the doors gave no indication of the tenants' names. The third, on which I subsequently knocked was, in contrast, covered with so many scribblings and drawings that it appeared even more anonymous. I thought that my master could well have hidden himself behind it: the interlacing words evoked an idea of blurred traces, of people being tracked. A young woman, short and pretty as far as I could tell against the light, opened the door. Behind her stood a boy wearing a large moustache. Already backing away, I named the person I was looking for as if to excuse myself for a mistake that seemed to irritate her more than was reasonable. 'Oh! You mean the lunatic,' the young woman said without any trace of a smile. 'One door over . . .' I grimaced the way one does on receiving a blow to the leg. She had immediately shut her door. When I knocked at the last of the three doors, on which I finally made out a large A, carefully painted but fading, I again heard no answer. I pushed open the door and saw the same dim light as in the room next door. I waited a moment. A voice said 'Come in,' but so softly that it could well have answered my earlier knocking without my hearing it. And right away, before I'd seen my master and as I turned towards the spot from which the voice had come, towards a sort of recess or alcove dimmer than the rest of the room, he added without any greeting, 'Have a seat,' pointing to a curule chair at a slight distance from the table, as if he had just pushed it back when standing up. My surprise was so sharp that at first I did not feel the dismay and sorrow his welcome unleashed in me. There were several minutes of silence. It gave me time to realize that the wretched building he had sought refuge in was one of those conglomerations of painters' studios, most of which were no longer in use and had been ceded to the poor families of which this neighbourhood was full. My master's studio was quite cramped and hardly merited its name except for the large window meant to illuminate it. Because his studio was on the ground floor at the far end of some kind of courtyard which was, in fact, not a real court-yard given that its base was not the ground but a large glass roof intended as shelter for garages or storage rooms, it seemed that all the dust from the upper floors had accumulated on the panes of glass. It was a winter evening; the light hid more than it revealed. Already I could barely discern anything close to the window, a long tabletop covered with various objects and the soft lustre of polish on the corner of wardrobe. As for my master, before I sat down as he had almost harshly requested, I'd just had time to make him out huddled on a narrow divan, like a mass of shadow—and mass is almost an over-statement—like some suspicious shadow that began to speak once my back was half-turned towards it in a voice even more muted than it had been in the past . . .

'You've arrived just in time: do not take your eyes off the window, if you please. In a few minutes you'll witness a spectacle that's at least worth announcing. We can speak in any case—the signal is silent at first.' So I sat facing the window; in other words, with my back to him, and I assumed these conditions were intended to make it easier for him to talk to me, as if I weren't there or as if my presence were simply a pretext, an encouragement, to soliloquize. I, myself, felt much more at ease this way, finding it so difficult to look at the incomprehensible misery into which he had sunk. The mere sight of him had brought home to me how silly the daydreams were I'd indulged in just moments before. He had not gone into hiding, holed up here in this room, for a rebirth—but out of despair. Was it to punish himself for having lived so brilliantly that he sought out this grave of a room in a neighbourhood of survivors, as in a fury one might extinguish a torch in mud? I listened to his words and truly believed I could see them plunge into the layer of ash, growing ever colder and darker, that obscured the window and I was reminded of those characters on stage who, when they disappear in a cloud of artificial fog, we know are headed towards their deaths.

'I had hoped you wouldn't find me, especially you, to whom I was so close and who had such faith in me. I'd have preferred to think you'd forgotten me or that you would remember me only as a happy, even triumphant man since that's how you knew me. But, I admit, your visit moves me, it does me good.

Maybe that's why I answered your note despite myself. Out of a need, vile but natural and irresistible, to talk—perhaps out of a kind of revenge, too. You'll understand me better later. I'm not asking for an answer, there is no answer to what I'm about to tell you. I'm not even asking you to pay attention, just to sit there with as much patience as your friendship for me can still muster so your presence will help some words rise into the air, words that would not otherwise have the strength, because this time, for once, they won't fall back into the absolute void that is my residence, my lair.'

As weary as his voice sounded, it had a shade of aggression I'd never heard in it before. I told him simply that I'd only come to help him, to listen to him, all night long if necessary. No doubt he remembered how I'd listened to him in this town at the time we first met, when he seemed a success in everything, even in an unhappy love affair. And in fact, after a movement that made the divan creak, he continued in the same vein: 'On your way here, you must have recalled our first meeting and what I confided to you later about my passion—my roving through the galleries along the river's edge almost twenty years ago—and here I am, back in this city to bury myself in this dusty rabbit hutch of a place, whose various goings-on you are about to witness . . .

'I can tell you what you're thinking: you're looking for a link between the ardent, feverish and sombre man I was then and the old man I've become, prematurely aged all the same. You won't find a link any more than I have, though for weeks now I've often asked myself, "Was it really me running down that street at night, fleeing the soirée's admiring murmur though without refusing its support, nonetheless feeling all the while a presentiment that some extraordinary possibility lay at the end of my flight?" How can I express this, I don't know, I've never known and, after all, it's no longer worth the effort . . . Would there have been the slightest difference if I'd read an account of this story in a book or if I'd dreamt it? How can I put it: it's inside me or just in my memory along with a thousand other foreign things, but more profoundly, more intimately so. How can I be sure that I didn't simply dream those alternations of light and shadow as the woman I loved and I passed the large pillars between vast bays that turned her now dark, now white as the moon itself, accompanied by the constant rumbling of passing cars, which I forgot only when she spoke or laughed, along with the sense I had (if it was, in fact, me) that *everything* depended on that moment (an absurd thought, really, a lie unworthy of a man)? Do we not experience, in dreams, visions and sensations every bit as precise, desires just as vast, and suffering that brings us to tears? Tell me, what difference is there between dream and memory considered from enough of a distance? Do you know how many months I followed her, how many hours I devoted to her even though I didn't love her nor did she love me, not even for a moment . . .'

I listened intently to the inflections in his voice. What struck me most, what I found painful, was that he didn't seem at all moved by remembering the past, as so many ageing men are. Instead, the only emotion able to turn him towards the past was a sense of resentment, of anger, the need to mock. 'You know that she was an actress, well, just a beginner, too young for the big roles but already surprisingly talented, perhaps because of her Slavic roots. It had nothing to do with professionalism or intelligence, but was all instinct, grace, because in every other way she was a child, as innocent as she was ignorant. And me with my gravity, my hidden fame, I followed her without telling her, from one country to the next, wasting money, sacrificing my work for the moment, so very brief, when she walked onto the stage—it always reminded me of those Balinese dancers sheathed in gold . . . Preceded by a music that was itself the sound of gold, they appeared in the opening of a narrow door set in the back wall of the stage set, a door the dancers reached by a staircase I believe, so that they only progressively became visible. And in the midst of the din, the clinking and jingling, the splendour, in what could recall the clashing of golden sabres (their flashing and slashing), what exactly was it? Their long, thin arms, their closed faces: suppleness, softness, a woman's voice calling incomprehensible words as a battle raged nearby . . . That must have been what I sought in her, the distant, the elusive. Naturally, the more she fled from me, the more I loved her. Sometimes, you know, I didn't have the strength to remain hidden until the end of the tour. I brought a jewel, flowers, to her dressing room and she received me with the barest surprise, with a laugh, as if it were natural that someone who loved her (and whom she saw as a brother, at times amusing, at others annoying) should follow her all over Europe. She was always tired but happy to have been on stage and I was exhausted by the waiting, the chase, the certainty that it was pointless and dread at the thought that once again we would only be together for a fraction of an hour. I was allowed to take her to a cafe, which pleased her no end—not because I was there but because my presence gave her an opportunity to prolong the evening, to get out in the world (her mother, whom we called Mene, was very strict). She would open her immensely large eyes even wider to better take in this new spectacle. Then I would leave the two of them, her and Mene, usually around midnight, on the doorstep of some brightly lit hotel, sometimes in the falling rain or occasionally snow or in the warm spring air. She answered my attempts to give her a sense of my inner devastation, my madness, with one last quip, a final laugh. She pressed herself gently against her mother and gave me a friendly wave, but a slight one, ever so slight, a flutter of wings. Then she did not turn around again . . .'

He must have been irritated with himself for giving way to emotion because he pulled himself together rather brusquely: 'No greater foolishness in the world. The millionth love story. Don't expect me to recount it from beginning to end. Ugh! Why linger one second more on these futile events, so unreal that I don't even know where they happened or if they actually happened to me? Is it possible that I truly believed the entire world was contained in such moments, that I *lived* because I ran, dreamt, trembled? As if to say: *I was alive?* What mad presumption. At the time, I was often convinced I was the unhappiest man on earth. What good is the gift of reason if you must indulge in such asinine illusions? Not unlike the whirls of dust motes I often see rising or falling outside these windows. Don't tell me that I amount to more than that, that I am anything more precious, more certain . . . Aha! You see? I didn't lie to you. Watch closely!'

The sort of rectangular well at the bottom of which we found ourselves was not completely enclosed. The tall building across from us, which opened onto the street and formed one side of the well, was separated from the neighbouring building by a gap of a metre or two, so that a vertical fissure formed between them, a kind of arrow-hole through which you could see, or at least discern, not only a fragment of the low facade across the street but also, above this facade and its roof, a strip of the sky. 'You see?' And, in fact, I did see a red torch pass over and even pause an instant over the slit, the low winter sun whose rays seemed too weak to penetrate into the room in which we sat. 'It's the announcer passing in front of the closed curtain, just before the stage lights up. The torch he carries is splendid, his gait harmonious and solemn. However, this spectacle's lights, strictly speaking, as you'll see, are spotlights that reveal nothing more than battles and battlefields, and not even real battles at that, but collisions, murders, ambushes.'

A vast bitterness seemed to inspire these images, images I understood very well as referring to what had begun to play out before my eyes, the curtain of obscurity now lifted—the spectacle that for many nights now he could not observe without sorrow. The studio windows that opened onto the wall perpendicular to his and the rear windows of the building that faced onto the street all lit up almost simultaneously once the sun had passed, although the shred of sky visible from the well was still light. Many of the windows had no curtains, at least, no one bothered to close any. The astonishing variety of life was displayed there. 'An unacceptable waste of gestures, of words, an incoherent mix of differences and similarities, endless complication, a boiler bursting with screams . . .' I don't know which I found more painful: seeing these vague silhouettes behind windows, some furtive, others immobile for long stretches of time (the studios were so small that empty windows were rare), each making its own gestures, imperfect, fragmentary, discordant, mysterious; or hearing that voice, barely audible and once in a while suddenly hard and almost shrill, commenting on the spectacle which, in truth, was no spectacle since these shadows were in all likelihood *alive*. 'Explain to me what difference it would make, not just in heaven but right here in this city, in this neighbourhood, on this street, if these really were just shadows. What need is there for this multiplicity of beings, for this proliferation of movements and words, for this infinite number of days, of objects, of stones? Couldn't God have preserved His unity? Remained God? No, He had to accept or provoke some kind of failure, after which He could only divide Himself ad infinitum, could only break apart.

Here we have, before our eyes, the putrefaction of the divine corpse—proliferation, liquefaction, vermin. Who raised his hand against this beautiful, intact sphere, this crystal ball, this sovereign globe? No one—had He tolerated the slightest mote of dust external to Him, He would no longer have been sovereign or perfect. Therefore, He carried His own death within—a seed, a simple grain that becomes a tree and hides within its closed husk not only thousands of leaves to come but also its lifespan and its end.

'This fumbling distress is no doubt hard for the heart to bear, but the spirit's futility is yet more so. The least of our labourers is less a bungler. I rarely go out any longer but each time I do, I have to negotiate these streets full of people, these long theories of dark souls, I realize you can't mention Hell without incurring their mockery because they are already there. All those beings, uglier than the most dispossessed of animals. Amid the crowds, where I should feel pity, I'm overcome with rage, not so much against injustice but against failure, the same way a schoolmaster who sees a notebook page full of ink blots and lines with each word written crookedly judges the student to be not quite normal. I study the faces avidly—you'd think not a day went by in which they were not abused, insulted, sullied, beaten, albeit less in the literal sense (though that happens too), than internally. Picture a young girl who is shown a marvellous doll, exactly the doll a little girl dreams of, and this girl is encouraged to long for the doll for months. And when the doll is finally given to her and she begins to play with it, the doll splits open down the middle, its insides teeming with vermin . . . But stop me—once you start down this road, there's no end. And, even though there are almost as many sad stories as there are residents in this abode, a mere ten of them, or perhaps even a single one, precisely recounted, is enough to reduce a man to the state I'm in. *This point proven*, can you justify such disorder? Some will no doubt claim that asking these questions will be your undoing . . . Right? I believe you do too, just as I myself have said in the past? But what is it that asks these questions when its happiness depends on not asking them, and who can stop it from posing more questions after the first one has been asked, after it is confronted with this spectacle or any other for that matter which, however monotonous, does not stop eliciting more questions? What is it that should not question yet can't keep from doing so? It seems to live from questioning, seems in fact to be a single continuous question, and yet questioning also seems an affliction for it? Come! Tell me what this obscure story means if you know, if you don't want to end up hiding yourself away in a corner as I have here, refusing to understand anything, unable even to begin understanding what is closest to me: my fingers, the embers in the stove, or the fog or a neighbour's shadow . . .

'I already know your objections: that my complaint is indecent, lacking courage and dignity, that I'm indulging in a lament while stringing words along, that I'm drowning in words, that as soon as one opens the door to questions and grievances, eloquence takes over and draws one away from truth; that one should be modest, ironic, virile, genial, saying only, *this is*, *that is not*. But that's cheating, or at least I would be cheating if I were to reject thus my life's fundamental truth—however dubious it may seem to me—to place it behind a wall or a screen and affirm that the only life is this lie, this forgetting or dodging of questions . . .'

'Oh! Did you hear that barking?'

This time the question was real, not rhetorical, conserving a silence that was immediately broken by a voice both aggressive and infinitely weary, flinging a single word through the layers of glass and cold, wintry fog: *Eat!* A vicious order, launched rather like an insult that relieves an extended humiliation, and indeed followed by a faint bark. I tried to discern which studio the sounds came from, surely one of the closer ones or we wouldn't have heard them. There was a window one floor above us, almost completely veiled by purple drapes while the harshly illuminated narrow strip was filled by a squat silhouette, that seemed folded in on itself, apparently facing the opposite corner of the room, which I could not see. *Eat*! Hearing the command again, more brusquely and ferociously delivered this time and in a higher register, I was certain that the silhouette had uttered it. 'For a long time, I thought that woman was talking to a dog or some other animal I pictured tied by a very short chain to the corner in her room that corresponds to the one I'm sitting in here. For several weeks I was fooled because even in daylight I could only see her standing near the window, just as she is now, leaning forward slightly next to the sink and because I only understood that one word you heard tear through the relatively silent courtyard twice just now and one other, *down*! or *lie down*!, along with a few curses that in this building are aimed indiscriminately at animals and people. The thought of her living with an animal obviously imprisoned seemed more and more dreadful, if not monstrous, and each time I passed the woman on the stairs or in the hallway—always walking quickly, her step more decisive than frightened and never furtive, her small face with its hardened, hollow features framed by short hair, her reddened complexion, her fixed gaze, her expression stony with hostility, always alone, always mute, never saying a word to anyone in this building where confabulations on doorsteps tend to go on and on—I became a bit more convinced that it was a dog she was taking care of, or persecuting, in this way. Besides, I sometimes heard the sound of barking, although very faint. However, it was that for all those weeks, her husband, her man, call him what you will, her beloved even, why not, was too sick to get up or even to speak, or perhaps too soaked in alcohol. Later, I happened to see him, too, in turn, on his feet but swaying behind the window. Then, one night not long ago (and maybe again tonight if you keep me company long enough), I even saw him, René is his name, taller than she is, with white hair even though he must only be in his forties, I saw him chase her making grunting noises that hardly resembled words. He held one arm out straight before him. I saw them pass in front of the window, then the window was empty and yellow again, then they reappeared. He obviously wanted to kiss her, to bring her to his bed despite their repulsiveness (the bed she only ever went near to hand him a plate he almost always pushed away), at which point I heard the crash of a plate breaking, almost immediately followed by sobbing and creaking from the bed onto which she must have managed to shove him and where he remained without any hope of gathering enough strength to get up again, at least not on that night, and carry out his plans, his dream . . . I think he's been in that room for several days now. From my room you can guess that his isn't large. There's not much air between us, you and me, not even when I'm huddled in my corner. So imagine if you were forced to live with me, even if only for twenty-four hours straight, separated by no more than two metres, within reach of each other . . . Why on earth is this facade ornamented by these two coupled bodies, what is the point of this grotesque projection into the architecture of a world you love so much? Explain their role and perhaps I will feel some solace. Nonetheless they are definitively, and in a sense eternally, essentially, fundamentally misplaced, impossible to place, incongruous and not only they, perhaps everyone else as well, I, too, in any case. I'm sure you understand what I mean. Oh, I'm weary. I'm disgusted to hear myself repeating yet again this inane complaint, true though it is and old as mankind: I'd promised myself I would remain silent rather than add another word . . .'

I was still not looking at him but, nonetheless, had the feeling I was seeing and touching him, the space that separated us was so slight, almost non-existent. And I knew him so well. The truth is, I would much rather have left. I was still young enough, still vigorous and fervent enough not to have forgotten all that the night in this city could offer even its most solitary residents: simply the lights over the terraces, the trees between the tall buildings and also, the opposite of his reaction, the multitude of faces, of lives, of dreams that became surprisingly tangible when I wandered along the avenues and boulevards at nightfall as I was fond of doing, satisfied with merely watching and imagining. Did this difference between us come down to the simple fact that I was younger than he, that, with luck, I could count on another forty years whereas the most he could hope for was twenty or twenty-five?

On the other hand, I knew very well I couldn't leave, not on that night. I knew he was counting on me and I was captive there as if he'd turned the key in the lock. This man had given me what reasons I had to live, had welcomed me into his home for months at a time. The least I could do, no matter how trying it became, was to listen to him break down and offer reasons to die. Fortunately, his neighbour's cries and the noises closer by of dishes and flowing taps had not only inspired in my master a surfeit of horror but also reminded him that the dinner hour was approaching. I wasn't very hungry, but the thought of sitting there for hours on an empty stomach made me apprehensive. He told me there was bread on the table, a bottle at the foot of the wardrobe and I should feel free to serve myself if my heart moved me. He himself hardly ate any more. 'I can barely keep down what I eat, just as I vomit up the world and these words.'

'But you. Don't pretend, it wouldn't be true. I'd be convinced of your bad faith if you could consider all this, look at it directly and still love your life. If you still have the slightest desire to live, it's because you turn away, one way or another (there are extremely subtle ways). I myself turned away for a long time, too, even though my whole life long I could feel inside, more or less deep within, more or less distant, some sort of terror or latent horror. But then I was able to forget it for months at a time— why? Thanks to what?'

At that moment I felt my attention sharpen with the presentiment that he was about to demolish the essential part of my relationship to him and of the lesson I believed I could draw from it: his former equanimity, more precisely, the kind of response to misfortune his life offered back then. At first, he remained silent for a long time; but I knew there was no risk he would fall asleep. I knew he was gathering his strength, as if mustering an army before a decisive attack. I was divided between dread, sorrow and mistrust. I told myself—though perhaps this was a way of securing my retreat, a way to avoid acknowledging defeat—that he would not back down before any lie, any distortion of his view, any alteration in the colour of things that might falsify the image preserved within me of those lucid moments, the blissful echo of his first words. Out of fear, I was pre-emptively defending myself against believing what he was about to say. The fire burnt weakly behind the stove's small glass door. The sound of the bread I chewed and the wine I poured had an insolent tone. The room was illuminated only by the light of the neighbouring studios. When I stood up to take the matchbox from the mantelpiece, I noticed I could barely stay on my feet, but this simple gesture freed me for a moment from the vertigo in which my master's monologue had plunged me. I sat down again, asking him to continue if it would do him good.

'Don't expect me to tell you everything when I would much prefer not to say anything at all.' He now lay fully reclined—I caught a glimpse of him from the corner of my eye when the curtain in a window of the building across us was abruptly pulled open and then immediately drawn shut again. Lying on his side, his head stretched out over the side of the bed, he made me think of someone leaning forward to speak into a hole in the ground and evoke the shades of the dead, although in his case you might wonder if he weren't trying to descend more quickly, to fall simply by looking into the depths.

'Of course, of course . . . Fragments of dreams, luminous debris. I know what you're thinking.' Lying there with his eyes fixed on the ground in a position that made speaking even more difficult, he looked as if he were about to summon who knows what shades from the dark and dusty abyss. He seemed to be spying into the darkness, digging into it like a dog scratching out a hole.

'What we call *signs*. Clear days, winged movements, words truly spoken. A few months of insouciance, of forgetfulness, perhaps. You met me at the right time, because lies are surely preferable to the truth—and the truth is that nothing is real, that *nothing is*, except for the evil of knowing this. If only this nothing were but a soft, downy absence, instead, it's a bristling, thorny, armoured nothing—sharpened blades onto which we are thrown and whose flashes sometimes delude us so completely that we believe we can make out celebrations, vast lakes . . . The famous signs. We are lured like birds—calls we imagine to be complicit lead us straight to our deaths. I came to this realization quite suddenly, for no apparent reason, the way you sometimes wake abruptly without knowing why. For several months, yes, I know, for several months I let myself go because of the woman you met, whom I charitably relieved of the burden of my company. With her, I believed I could live, I mean live with dignity, that it would be worth the trouble, all I had to do was make the effort and a bit of patience and courage would suffice. Suffice for what? I myself wasn't quite sure, but it didn't matter, the illusion was so comforting.

Suffice, perhaps, to understand suffering, multiplicity, change, to resuscitate God, without whom I no doubt couldn't manage—like most people. Whereas, in fact, patience, virtue and courage only ever suffice to lead us to death, like crime.

'It's the horror of the void that leads us all and that's why we should be wary of theories that tend to deny, hide or span the void—we are too invested in their success. We will think up any scheme—you know this even if you'd rather not—we will resort to the most unlikely subterfuges (even the most honest, the bravest among us) to do away with this void by whatever means possible. Because thinking it is impossible, as is living it—I have become proof of this. What have we done, you and I, of the time when you lived with us, when we abandoned ourselves without a second thought to the "joys of nature", when I thought there was only one path for all of us even if the world were breaking apart? *Our ancestors, the Gauls, feared but one thing: that the sky would fall on their heads*—one of the first truths we were taught at school. Well! There we were and the distant descendants of these fearless, unreproachable heroes finally understood that this phrase did not mean the Gauls feared no real dangers, but that they feared, they dreaded the one true danger, the one that several centuries later would become the source of widespread terror. How many times have I not dreamt since those years of respite that the order of heaven had collapsed: the most terrifying thought of all . . . One time, for example, I stood by the French door in the living room of our family home, admiring the sight of the sun setting between the trees in our garden. I was overcome with a sense of astonishment, which quickly turned to fear, because five or six concentric circles formed around this sinking orb as I remembered seeing in pictures of certain meteors, all of which interested me intensely. Hesitating was not possible for long, so I set to observing the spectacle ever more intently. It turned into a desert of blinding light above which or in which the sun's disc and a single star were still visible (except, perhaps, for one or two branches in the foreground, as black as the balcony ironwork). I took a sheet of paper and wrote hastily, while there was still time, the words *star*, *desert*, *sun*. I might have been able to bear the sight of this dazzling expanse but, as if I were not meant to harbour any illusions, details appeared in the expanding fire that resembled the inside of an oven: tall buildings on the left and in the centre, like a brand new toy, a red bus that collapsed from the back as if it were *melting*, which it no doubt was. So I ran to the other end of the house to get further away from this spectacle. I entered a room that struck me as strangely grey and in which worse yet awaited me. My son sat in the room wearing a black cape that gave him the air of both a penitent and a bat. My wife lay prostrate, irritably lethargic. My mother was searching for a balm she'd been told was protective so she could spread it on the child's legs . . .

'I could recount many such dreams, all of them forcefully demonstrating that, even when happy, we lived in a world in which stone can melt, seas can spurt all the way up to the sky, our most cherished, most secret refuges turn to ash in the space of a sigh. It's true that at the time I'm describing, I quickly forgot such dreams for immediate joys or worries. Perhaps these nightmares seemed to me one more reason to cling to such moments, to signs, to transitions. There is the void that, one day or another, in one way or another, is discovered and experienced as emptiness and, in addition, there was, ever since the war years—during which you yourself were only a child and therefore escaped them—blinding evidence of the void that threatened us. There are signs and promises, after all. The time to gather these famous signs, to protect them from the encroaching void was thus long overdue. It was time to found upon them, as a last resort, some system capable of rigging truth one last time, capable, in other words, of subsuming the void or making it seem a source of plenitude . . . That's the task we set ourselves and we certainly thought we were sincere: facing our dishonesty would have meant facing the fact that the only thing guiding our thoughts and acts was fear of the void.

'It's natural that youth is more easily fooled because it has some characteristics of the harmony we dream of. Its beauty, its strength, resemble the beauty and strength of the gods we want to be. Love is a moment in a divine story, illuminated by an unknown star. The first grey hair dethrones us and reveals that death was within us all along. An infinite sadness invades the divine palace like a fog at summer's end that gradually shrouds the landscape in successive, lingering bands. Don't go looking for the cause of my fall, which must appear more sudden to you than it actually was, in the days' secrets and especially not in those of the night where too many curious people, stupefied by false information, are rushing to intrude. I could have kept on living with that woman, so patient, so undemanding, so cheerful and raising the child whose irreplaceable grace I saw more clearly than anyone else. Other men manage to do this. I also seemed, resolute as I was, destined to succeed. And after all, wasn't it a sacred duty as they say?'

Again he remained silent for a long time, as if he really were considering the question and his possible guilt or perhaps simply because he was overcome with fatigue. As for me, I was exhausted from the

sadness, the discomfort, the strain of paying attention. I had seen the lights in the windows go out one
after the other, except for one or two. The facades
behind these windows would soon be nothing more
than expanses of shadow in varying shades of black.
The glass ceiling over the basement gleamed in spots.
I asked permission to light the candle I'd noticed on
the mantelpiece, left there no doubt for the power
failures that were frequent in these old buildings. Its
thin glow was just enough to cover the light from
outside and the room seemed slightly less cold, less
miserable. My master's bed, however, retreated into
shadows made more opaque and, from then on, with
every answer, every echo to my words, all I had
before my eyes were a few objects scattered over the
table: my dirty, empty wine glass, my plate, a small
platter holding pencils, pens, pins and coloured
stones. There wasn't a single book to be seen, but
there were newspapers stacked in a corner. And if I
turned away, I could see, above the almost purple
embers in the stove, the reflection of the candle in the
dusty mirror shining like a fiery blade as well as, on
the mantelpiece, a pocket knife, a lead fork and a pair
of pliers. My master's voice had begun to rise again,
to envelop me as it were. I thought of something that
had occasionally happened to me as a child. Doing my
homework, all of a sudden I'd hear, I'd sense very near
me, next to my ear, not so much a conversation as a

hurried murmur, as if several extremely agitated, perhaps anxious people were whispering to one another, sometimes all at once. In any case, I couldn't hope to understand what they were saying and that's what I found so frightening. I would shake my head and try to get rid of the murmuring, but that was impossible. It never went on for very long and only ever ended of its own accord. But this time, I understood all too clearly the words buzzing around my head and I had the feeling that the words I'd heard as a child had only intimated what I now would have to endure without being any better able to put an end to it.

'It's merely time that ruined me. The reason is simple: you don't have to round up a pack of wise men to understand what happened to me. Every mature man has skirted this abyss with his eyes wide open. There's a time when we can speak of death as a terrible threat. Then the time comes when death is lived, so to speak, as that which will destroy life from this moment on. These two experiences are completely disproportionate. After having at first appeared to be a source of light—you remember, that's how we thought of it?—death becomes an absolute darkness. Then one's momentum snaps like a violin string. And thus, disoriented, we drift from one thought to the next, looking for rescue but we reject all ideas as if they, too, had been rendered inane. When you knew me, I was still a young man—when young, we're protected by a future which, to be sure, we don't believe is unlimited but we *feel* to be so. Then the future suddenly disappears, seems non-existent, even though the number of years we can reasonably hope to live has not diminished all that much. I've never experienced a worse moment. In fact, I'm probably already dead or started dying that very moment. Back then, nights were the worst, when I would hear the bird of night call like a jailer whistling in the narrow corridor between two rows of cells.

'All that we once thought about the solace of the visible world, all we once said about submission to the order of the world, about accepting limits, seemed to me too easily said, too readily believed. Not even love or smiles were able to preserve me. Perhaps one day I might have been able to take up the fight once again, to continue the search, in another sense, to defy the void. You think I should have. But that's because you haven't yet lived through that moment, you're moving forward with your eyes closed and what I'm telling you right now can't open them for you. A profound experience can't be completely communicated—the essence of it remains inaccessible. There is a kind of night we can't describe but have to enter to recognize that it is bottomless  and without end. That's why the writings of philosophers and saints strike me as useless: reading them, meditating on them, even with close attention, brings us only a bit more knowledge as long as we have not lived through their experiences ourselves—which is, in any case, impossible. That is also why man never makes real progress internally . . .

'How is it that I didn't look for another way out? Because I believed I'd investigated every one? No. It was because seeking or not seeking was, in my eyes, all the same ever since I'd understood or, rather, experienced the force of time. I could perceive the urgency of some certitude but, at the time, it seemed equally improbable. Everything became more acute, in one sense, but everything became more blunt as well because, in any case, the only one winning was time. Each question I would have to take up once again only shortened the brief interval that remained for me. Time advanced like fire through dry grass. It floored me. I often repeated to myself the words of the poet: *if I were offered a choice between the fortune and glory of Caesar or Alexander, both free of any taint, or dying this very day, I would say, "dying this very day" and would make my choice without any hesitation.* The phrase "dying this very day" is absurd, for that matter, because that is what we do from the moment our eyes are opened to the reality of the void. There was no longer any choice: I could have chosen any-thing whatsoever, let's say glory and fortune to keep it simple, and in all my glory and fortune, I would be no less dead each day. Is there anything more easily understood, anything so crudely, so monstrously clear? I wanted to hide this truth, which I could feel was already altering my features, giving me the face of an old man, the eyes of one condemned. And yet, it wasn't easy . . . I would secretly watch my wife and my child. I tried to take up again my walks along familiar paths. I simply couldn't understand how people and things that had once been so close to me, so invaluable, could, almost from one moment to the next, seem so utterly distant. No doubt I could have pretended that nothing had changed. I thought it best to submit to the cruel truth of such moments and accept the consequences. A spectre flees daylight—if he wants to warn the living, we know that he must do so, as on this night, in the dark.

'And now I'm so weary that I beg you, as if it were a last request, to stay with me until daylight dispels me. I won't keep you awake if you want to sleep, but stay at my side for a time yet if you are to be the last man whose presence I will have felt in this world. My words can't help me, true, but I've unburdened my spirit. And now you see that the lights outside have all been turned off. No doubt all the building's residents are asleep, except for one or two who, like me, are kept awake by the thought of the prodigious error in which they've been caught, or less than a thought—the very apprehension, at night's deepest hour, of the void. Often, back then, I would stretch out my hand and grasp my companion's wrist as if, even asleep, she could keep me from falling. It's a moment when there is no longer the slightest noise, not a glimmer except for the dullest gleam, a moment without end. And then I'd hear the first rooster crow, that cry always seemed to me to be more of a call for help than one of triumph: as if a soul struggling with this vision of despair without borders or limits, had understood that nothing less would chase it away than the invention of the sun. And yet, when this vision engulfed even the light, then one knows there is no longer any hope of a handhold. Nevertheless, it's true that I did notice certain flowers . . .'

He fell silent so abruptly that, struck as I was by the tenor of his statements, I shuddered, fearing he might actually have died. But I immediately heard the breathing of someone sleeping. It was as if an enormous burden had fallen from my shoulders; I was suddenly sure that I would not have been able to bear the weight even a second longer. I pushed aside the plate that still lay before me on the table and rested my head on my crossed arms, hardly daring to hope I'd manage to doze off, especially since the room had become extremely cold. Still, I believe I did fall asleep because what I now recall of those moments is a swarm of nightmarish images, inseparable from the room I was in and the words I'd had to listen to. At one point I saw myself in a car with my master driving along a mountain road bordered by steep pastures. In the middle of one of these pastures stood a tall stone, which was a woman, a woman turned to stone, who could only be freed from the spell by true love. I remember being hesitant to save her. I felt a vague but immense desire for this woman I didn't know. In the sky above the mountains there was an elaborate constellation of new stars, black discs, fiery trails, and we left the woman with the thought that if she remained stone, she would see such wonders in the centuries to come it would be well worth the enchantment. But as we drove away, one of the many flocks of birds we'd seen swirling above our car as we ascended began attacking our windows and we were convinced we would not make it out alive.

When I awoke, exhausted, nauseous, chilled, I heard the blare of a car's horn that seemed to come from some distance away, from one of the ring roads or bypasses beyond which the nondescript suburban zones begin, towards which the car must have been headed, its headlights still on but not for much longer. For a moment, I followed it in my mind (the sky must have brightened a bit, almost imperceptibly, the silence in the courtyard was still absolute, that most difficult time of day prolonged itself through a hint of grisaille along the walls that resembled an assault of fog rather than the break of day), my thoughts followed the car (my face literally turned towards the direction the sound had come from) to the point where, leaving the suburban houses and factories behind, it would be surrounded only by fields and the vast silvery sky. Then I discreetly turned away from the window, but sensing there was something in the far corner, something even darker than the shadows that still shrouded that part of the room, a kind of shrivelling or concentration of nocturnal shadows, I didn't have enough courage to fix my eyes on the one who had in the meantime awoken and was speaking again (but had he truly slept, had he actually fallen silent?) in his inexhaustible whispering desolation, but he was now completely oblivious to my presence and to his own, to everything around us that might be seen, heard or experienced. I'd never been able to endure sleepless nights, even the happiest ones. I must have been pale. The last audible noises had been the squeaks of my chair, the creaking from the bed and, at ever greater intervals, the hissing from the fire dying in the stove as in a small cast-iron altar and, very occasionally, steps in the street that always sounded rushed, limping, frightened.

'. . . The depth of night. We need words to describe those moments, not just any words, not some simple clamour to distract or destroy thought but a kind of prayer—words carefully chosen and arranged so that they will give measure to this void, simple reference points that will keep us from going astray. Certain words seem to provide direction. No one knows exactly how. And so we imagine they will lead us out of the void—that is a mistake, but the void is unbearable. In the past, men had such assistance, even or especially the simplest among them. They were concerned not only with building roads and inns in the world of appearances—some of the happiest moments in my old life, for that matter, the memory has returned suddenly and with particular force, were the times we said goodbye outside the refuge with the car's headlights still lit because of the early morning fog . . . They also showed ways through the void, that is, through the real. They illuminated paths, rivers, streets, intersections. They invented carts or small boats to navigate them. They said: *Keep going until you see a large cypress and the stone of Persephone* . . . They knew which instruments eased the way through this obscurity; they even made blood flow or milk, they mixed elemental scents; for the garb of messengers, guides and judges, they combined certain colours, certain designs that also seemed capable, through some complicity with the depths, of orienting lost and frightened souls. It took centuries to develop this knowledge of relations with the void, of charting paths through the dark. A knowledge lost in acquiring others that only increase our sense of terror . . . Year after year, with a steadily increasing rapidity, progressing along a course that can only lead to a rupture in our sense of measure, we have lost sight of those supports it is very much in our interest to safeguard. We may also convince ourselves that we were not the ones who destroyed them or left them behind, that things developed differently, followed a course that was much less dependent on human will than we believe . . .

'As for us, we who are now so proud of our power over appearance, if we encountered the void again, what power would we have over it? We have no reason to dread either the moaning, feeble pale shades who regret the daylight or those monsters, still so alive in their nine circles of hell. All those images have vanished. What we confront is no longer night, no longer that vague obscurity in which I find myself, no longer the dust on a bronze lock, in the depths that are not depths any more, no more shades, no longer a warm hole in the earth. To say all this is nothing is to say too much. Keeping silent is not silence enough and taking an eraser to rub out the lineaments of this world is not enough, only this gesture still full of gentleness, change and promise. To be sure, we're aware that there are churches and systems, we can study them as we study those objects we see gleaming in museum display cases, bits of jewellery, shards of pottery and armour covered with verdigris. All this does not prevent me from being cut off, terribly cut off, moved, perhaps, but in a sterile way. I cannot enter those shelters conceived for the men of old—if I do enter, I have no place there. At a certain moment, I wake from this reassuring dream, I open my eyes and feel as if I'm suspended, waiting, fed only with uncertainty and apprehension. And that's why I didn't think of lighting the lamp. No lamp can light my way or, if it could, what it revealed would be much worse. Just as should daybreak persist in coming, I would only understand all the more clearly the extent of my abandonment—I would see only strange faces, empty forms, false directions, deceptive or useless clarity, situated haphazardly around me, ground that no longer supports me, a bed on which I can no longer lie down, walls that don't prevent anything from coming near or evading me, this self with whom I can scarcely identify. All that's left are these words, like the puffs of smoke dervishes in Arab tales conjure up when they want to disappear and, indeed, in their ever more hurried movement these words preserve me in their fashion even if they can't save me. I chose them too rashly, you see, or, on the contrary, too carefully perhaps, using them, like you, in an attempt to escape one last time, aware of the futility but still sensitive to the suffering this escape entails. I am like a cuttle-fish at the bottom of my dark aquarium, puffing out clouds of even darker words, hiding behind them and still breathing or panting only thanks to them.'

At that point my master seemed to be trying to catch his breath. Morning had yet to break, perhaps because the sky had become overcast during the night and because the sun rises late this time of year. Trying desperately to resist the temptation of falling back asleep—which would have had the added ben-efit of sparing me the trial of listening to him—I saw my master sit up awkwardly on his bed. From the corner of my eye, I watched him shift his body as if to stand, but his strength failed him and he sat with-out moving in a position that looked so uncomfort-able, I couldn't help but wonder how he kept himself from swaying or tipping forward and reflected that I myself could never have held that position. He started speaking again, trying to brighten his voice but unable to manage anything more than a murmur, a jerky and occasionally almost spiteful murmur.

'Still, I want to make one more effort (why, I don't know, for my honour, maybe, in a world where honour means nothing, or, rather, in defiance, knowing that such defiance is completely pointless) to choose my words in the vague hope that instead of obscuring what I feel, they will clarify it, name it, shrink it (what a foolish, absurd hope). All the while I act like a soldier, which is quite ironic given what I am . . .' I thought then that on the contrary there was, indeed, an irrepressible trace of hope in him, one he could not acknowledge, that had to be what I was seeing, but he didn't leave me any time to consider it more closely.

'And yet, I doubt I have enough strength left. I've been weighed down by fatigue for a long time now and every day the weight grows heavier, as if to take away this last chance to speak a few honest words. And if I try to overcome the fatigue, to pull myself together, a veil envelops my thoughts, suffocates them and clouds my vision—a merciful veil, perhaps . . .

'I lack the courage, the determination—that's what you're thinking, isn't it, even though you don't dare say so? But does anyone ever associate courage with complete lucidity? Who, that is, what sensible man only slightly above an animal, could squarely face the spectacle he's been dealt and not falter? As for me, you see, all my protections were taken from me one after the other. I remember we agreed in our conversations years ago that it would be better to remain silent than add a single word to the darkness of human lives, but at a certain point I lost the ability to utter one clear word and yet I still could not resign myself to silence. Silence always descends soon enough. It's difficult to accept anything that scorns clarity after you've experienced such vivid, transparent clarity.

'Now, what's going to happen now, that's what constantly fills my thoughts. With what can I counter this great mass of the unknown that's drawing near, this imminence of the intangible? Do not claim that I might not be conscious at the right moment since the process has already begun, it began a long time ago, and as the moment approached with longer, more confident strides, I felt more disarmed, more unsure, for all the value certain people ascribed to my life before. No doubt age is kind in that it detaches us from life, from this earth, as we near the end and as for me, overnight or just about, I felt as removed from life as I'd believed I was close to it when I was a young man who believed that closeness would last forever. But when all these ties, even the most tenuous, are broken, how can we stand this floating between the world and the void and the humiliation of an ordeal in which we're reduced to complete incapacity?

'You pity me for being utterly alone, mistakenly discounting your own presence as insignificant. No doubt . . . in any case, the distance is infinite, you understand, perhaps even more awfully tangible. If I had a hand to hold, the hand of someone with whom I'd shared many of my days and the earth's air, it would be all the more repugnant: if only because of the thoughts that fill the heads of the living about what they will do the next day, the next month, the coming years and my complete inability to preserve the slightest trace of them in me . . .

'One last thought of this world? That's what you're recommending for me, isn't it? A fond goodbye to the best days? But it's only the living who harbour the idea that even one pleasant thought will remain to the dying. Listen closely but don't believe what I say lest you despair too soon: fate's cruellest trick is the shadow that projects intimations of mortality on the clearest fragments of our past. Suppose I wanted to oppose, making a sudden effort, the place towards which I'm heading with some marvellous memory (assuming I could, of course, which is impossible). No matter how carefully I looked, even if I wiped my eyes, what would I see besides a few disfigured moments, unreal landscapes, traces of gestures, confused, muddled faces? Maybe you're the one I should ask to bring these moments closer to me, to revive them, you, who have not seen them distorted by time as I have. You'd say: Wasn't it on that night in March that the sight of the river, sparkling and dark, raised you above all your fears, all obstacles, even though you'd been abandoned by the woman you'd been pursuing, even though you remained motionless, leaning against a column covered with names of people long dead? . . . Wasn't it one autumn ten years ago, an autumn so clear, so soft it seemed as if not only time were suspended but all puffs of air as well, that you believed, just by looking at those who would share your life from then on, that you held in your hands a treasure able to render any threat powerless? Didn't you say you couldn't possibly imagine life apart from this woman, this child, this countryside which the willows were beginning to illuminate with their flames and where we waited for the jays' faithful passage, where, at night, we discovered Orion rising above the horizon, heralding the first chill? Me, I would listen to your recitation as if to a charming tale, a story intended to soothe childish fears, in any case as if it all had happened to someone else because all I can see from the hole I'm in is a repulsive and incomprehensible whirl of dust motes, scraps of aborted stories, nothing, at any rate, that could pacify even the least demanding heart . . .

'You say nothing, you're no longer thinking: and in this you're nearing the place I am in now. And here I am, muttering into the void with a barbarian's panic and a barbarian's reactions, foolish, humiliating but still irresistible—like the ancient need to offer something to the judge to mollify him, win him over, to give an offering to the ferrier of souls even though I know perfectly well that there are no souls, no river, no ferryman. I would not make a good impression, faced with the Intangible One. For days now, I have been turning in all directions, in search of what? A gift for Him, a gift so marvellous, so dazzling that He, like the sultan before the goblet unveiled by Aladdin's mother, would smile at me and descend the steps of the throne before me. (You see how the images mislead, deceive, how, in the images, I flee the threat of their disappearance!) All the same, if only there were some indication hidden in this idea of *bedazzlement:* a way to absorb the obscurity in the brilliance or to insert a kind of glittering blade into it and dissect or dislocate it? . . .

'I've tried to bring together the remote fragments of my life, to revive forgotten words or smiles. I should have been able to assemble them into a sort of bouquet as proof that I hadn't always succumbed to his power, that I hadn't refused or neglected certain gifts. I couldn't make them cohere. All that was near me, all that I found at hand were those sad faces passing like the dead over the dusty mirror of those windows. The only things near me were dark emanations from the void. But in speaking to you this way, I'm once again letting illusions lead me astray. That's all we really do, as you know. We've never stopped being frightened children who are told stories or invited to play games to distract us from our fears . . .'

In spite of my drowsiness, I noticed he was breaking off more frequently than he had earlier in the evening but for shorter periods of time. He seemed to be on the edge of exhaustion but feared more than anything else a silence from which he would not have the strength to re-emerge, a silence in which he might be lost for good.

'Nevertheless, I made an effort. I didn't keep what energy and time I had for myself alone. I tried not to cause only harm. Once or twice I spoke words so clear that I hoped they would carry me like rafts. I had to fight not only against my weakness or selfishness but also against the world outside, its harshness, its constant ferocious effect on everything I tried to undertake. Will that change the weight of my ashes at all? There is no passage from the known to

the unknown: that is the last truth it seems I was able
to reach as I collapsed. As a result and since the two
are so disproportionate, the balance of the former
breaks down before the latter and, no matter what I
did, far from accessing this disproportion calmly or
even with joy, I only collided with it as violently as
before.

'Yes, that may well be true (although nothing
can be said to be true or false in this extremity, but I
am necessarily speaking of what precedes death). I
am nearing the place in which everything is reversed
and confused, in which it is impossible to orient one-
self. Already—and this is strange, given that I am
not at all ailing—I've been taken an incalculable distance from the earth. I'm searching for a comparison
that would make this sensation clear, but I can't find
any that are precise enough or strong enough. I'm
talking about *something* whose immediacy spreads
disorder to its surroundings, the mere thought of
which is enough to disrupt thought and perhaps even
suspend it completely. You've built a house and suddenly find yourself thrown down where there isn't
even any ground to dig a foundation. You've been a
body with its humours, you've made your peace with
it as best you could, and now no longer have a body,
no sight . . . You've suffered, borne your suffering
in the belief that suffering elevates, ennobles, but
what if there is nothing left that even resembles

suffering? You see, no matter how I search for words, they're always wide of the mark, never accurate. The truth, you understand, is that I cannot *pass*, there's nothing I can do, I'm always blocked . . . and should a sensible man accept this rebuff, this end? . . .

'I do not accept that I've been given the power of thought only for it to be destroyed by the inevitable impact against this wall. If one day my thinking should drift, should panic, whatever order it has been able to establish would be nullified. It had to stay the course until the very end, to resist anything that would definitively prevail over it, or else everything it has constructed is nothing but illusion, falsehood. That is true death—the moment when one's spirit, in colliding with the impossible, sees everything that had happened until then suddenly crumble: fame, happiness, greed, violence, standing still or walking, work or contemplation. Everything sinks into the void, into the inexpressible, into that for which the words *desert*, *darkness*, *void* are much too flattering.

'Must we then have lived this life, a life we hardly feel we actually lived, must we have passed through this unreality only to arrive at this horrible moment in which reality and unreality merge? Must we rid ourselves of everything but the sentiment of life's nullity? Must we discover life's insignificance and experience no less forcefully the panicked, visceral horror at the prospect of being torn from this nothing? Must we struggle and at times endure unbearable suffering only to reach this culmination of grief, this void that reveals everything around us to be nothing more than emptiness cloaked in appearance? If I had a taste for violence, if I still had a little life left in me, I would start beating my fists against this thin partition wall—you would hear what a hollow noise it makes. Bruising my fists to make the void resound—an apt image for our works. The black void of these hallways onto which our rooms open, along the entire lengths of these halls you will encounter only shades, because you will leave me now. No doubt you will have to walk down those roads again where I see only faces reproaching me for what little life I have left.

'A handful of dust swept together ... Was it necessary for this dust to suffer so much from existence? To cause so many difficulties? Please forgive me.'

The room suddenly seemed to light up from within: it had started to snow. The candle on the mantelpiece was still burning. Far from meditating on what my master had just said, far from rushing to his bedside and helping him or intervening in some way or other—all of which would have been perfectly natural—I was later surprised to realize I had simply sat there, transfixed, as if hypnotized by the glow that persisted at the centre of another dimmer glow. It wasn't very bright at all, in fact, but it was so vast it seemed without limit. I don't believe I thought anything particularly precise at the time, but I watched the flame shining in the breaking day with the intensity of someone scrutinizing a vision in order to be able to envision it clearly enough to understand it after it disappears. At most, in that instant, I might have had some thought of relay, of transmission or of passage, but it was more emotion than thought and, surprisingly enough, given the glacial cold in the room and the sinister circumstances, it was an almost joyful emotion, obscurely joyful, which, moreover, I would only recall much later. Then, just when I was about to stand up to blow out the candle (and, in fact, to hide my dismay and complete ignorance as to what I should do next), I heard the words: 'We definitely have a new day. Flee this place, I implore you: not that you're a spectre exposed to the dangers of daylight, but to avoid seeing one whom light might not disintegrate. Do not turn around, just open the door and close it carefully behind you. Hurry, go quickly, for the love of . . .'

I wish I could say that I hesitated before obeying him. Perhaps I did, I'm not sure. Those words rang in my ears with great force and bore an authority that seems almost incredible to me now. What's more, I'd lost all courage at the time, all presence of mind. It was as if the darkness of the room in which I'd spent the night and the deeper darkness evoked by his stifled voice had finally reduced me to nothing more than a shade with only shadowy emotions I could not translate into action. And so it was something of a chance for me, unmoored as I was, to be given this strange, cruel order and all that was left for me to do was to obey hastily as in a dream. I did not turn my eyes in his direction (I wonder now what I would have seen in the corner where he sat since the light had by then reached his lair for the first time since I'd arrived) and I closed the door behind me still without thinking (without daring to think), whereas I should have been burning with shame and regret. The building's hallways were still plunged in darkness and I was struck by the penetrating odour of urine wafting through them. When I stretched my hand out towards the wall in an attempt to orient myself or at least to avoid stumbling over any stairs, I felt the dampness of the plaster against my palm. Then, in the utter silence, I thought I saw a white shape approaching—it was the glimmer of snow in the entryway.

I walked for a long time through streets just beginning to waken while the sky cleared and the last traces of snow faded on the sidewalk. It had been one of those big-city snows, so humid that it turned to water or mud as soon as it touched the ground. I still gave no thought to what I'd heard and certainly not to what it could mean for my master and for me, who had placed all my confidence as well as my immense admiration and hope in him for so long. All I had was a buzzing in my ears, more insistent than the whistling sound of passing cars, like a funeral dirge or the whispering of spectral voices—threatening, scornful, maudlin—that seemed to want to keep me from hearing anything other than sarcastic remarks or complaints; and even though I was climbing as I approached my hotel, I couldn't help but see the city retreating little by little and spreading out before my eyes, and its tallest buildings began glittering in the pink sunlight as they emerged from the fog that still covered the suburbs and the horizon, all the while feeling as if a cloud of ash enveloped my head. More than anything else, however, it was his voice that persisted, growing stronger as my exhaustion grew. Before reaching the esplanade above which I would finally be able to collapse onto my bed and, with luck, fall asleep, I had the impression—utterly absurd but extremely intense—that his voice was a furious scratching of nails on the city—which I could now see in almost its entire expanse, dusty, golden, beneath a immense, crystalline sky—a scratching that erased everything, lacerated everything, so that even the highest sections of air crumbled, dust onto dust. The murmur's echo had barely reached my ears even though they'd been very close to the mouth that produced it and yet it was a murmur powerful enough, you could say, to bury an enormous, noisy city and even this vast sky in which I'd long seen the future's weightless image.

**II**

Recovering from the blow I suffered that night required a great deal of effort. I had seen a sensitive man, full of energy and with a perfect balance of intelligence and passion, prudence and hope—a man who I felt, the moment I met him, was made for a full life, for success, a man I believed would always rise, would escape the decline which threatens almost everyone else—end up like a miserable wretch repudiating what he had praised with so much conviction. He was the one who taught me to love life. Together we'd resolved never to add a single complaint to human unhappiness. We wanted, instead, to act, to talk and to live only to communicate to others the light with which we felt we were surrounded. It's not that shadows seemed unreal to us, or suffering derisory, or evil non-existent or insignificant—we saw far too much of these. In fact, we believed horror was steadily proliferating. Yet precisely that—our deep disgust for vulgarity, for foolishness, for the reigning ferocity—is what made us resolve to side with clarity. Not once did we think of turning our backs to misery (and how could we have, since it was deep within us?). Not once did we dream of leaving this world. It simply seemed to us that despite the spread of evil (obvious and certainly monstrous), the accelerated expansion of its power, 'something' in each of our lives opposed this growth, balanced it somewhat (and yet . . .). It must have been a miracle of sorts, a mystery in any case, because it had no authority, it was precarious, elusive; nonetheless, it did battle with horror, it didn't evade the horror but seemed to promise the possibility of victory. It was a wonderful opening . . . at the same time, it was the source of all happiness; it fed our actions and our dreams; it was a daily defiance of degradation and death.

Neither he nor I, nor his companion once he no longer lived alone, were religious. Yet what for us surely took the place of prayer with each new dawn was the thought of this promise which was not made by a god or made in any language of this world and which no book or system of reasoning could have guaranteed; the thought that, despite appearances that became more adverse, more harrowing with each year—because already back then the cataclysm could be concealed within the smallest grains or seeds, in small shiny things seen passing through the air like drops of water—everything was not futile, not immaterial, that there was good and evil, even if they weren't exactly what others believed or claimed they were. There was, therefore, in a certain sense, a high and a low, the possibility of leading our lives according to what exalted us, of avoiding or rejecting what abased us. We kept smiling, we felt very brave and didn't shirk any of the tasks or the many diverse obstacles life imposes on human beings. I had based my life on this presentiment and nothing had been able to destroy or even shake it. Yet he who illuminated its meaning for me, for whom it had been a much more reliable guide, he who I'd believed was so much better prepared to follow orders or advice, poised to follow a magnificent trajectory up until the day he would die in absolute serenity—like one who never stops hoping for yet more light—he had, in the end, and I could not understand why, repudiated it all, had lost it all. He had collapsed. I had just heard him moan interminably like those he'd so often excoriated in front of me, with me. I thought I'd never heard a more desolate lament—his disillusionment was as abrupt as his hope had been fervent.

I realized that I was going to have to endure long months with this lamentation ringing in my ears and that it could drag me into a deep hole like a weight too heavy to bear. In fact, it seemed to me—am I wrong to confess it?—more serious, if not more piteous than the one I might have heard that same night, if I'd been more attentive, from the mouth of a sick man, a miserable or tortured man. I had the impression I'd heard a god lamenting, admitting that his divinity was a mere reflection or mirage that would end with him. As excruciating as some forms of suffering can be, that one was perhaps the worst. Shouldn't I have thought of Christ at that point and heard in his agonized cry the lamentation of the last of the gods?

What my master said that night, what he tried to make me understand, was ultimately that the light we glimpsed and pursued so ardently was just one illusion among many, destined, perhaps, to help unhappy human beings caught up in a long and incomprehensible history better endure their thankless role. It was indeed possible, or should one say tempting, to describe human history as the gradual unveiling of a number of illusions (an unveiling considered progress by some, a catastrophe by others)— men had believed there were gods in trees and in stones, then they placed them ever higher, on mountaintops, in the sky, as if to ensure that their existence could never be verified or their absence confirmed. Men had believed the world was the centre of the universe, only to see it dethroned. They had judged their nation or their race invincible and superior to all others (sometimes finding enough strength in this illusion to vanquish much larger and more powerful armies). After travel and study clarified their knowledge, they understood that other civilizations had shone among men (as other suns shine in the sky), they lost the strength and taste for warring with other civilizations and soon declined from an excess of wisdom and justice, yielding to peoples still ignorant enough to believe themselves endowed with sacred missions. They had believed their work eternal and discovered its precariousness little by little. Recognizing that their bodies were perishable, they imagined their souls to be immortal, then trembled to see it deteriorate from a simple sting. Upon each of these upheavals, as profound as they were obvious, everyone said: the truth about mankind is emerging step by step from the veils that concealed it. Whereas some rejoiced, proclaiming that the illusions had only misled mankind and hindered his progress, others looked on in horror, perceiving a pure nothingness at the core of this naked truth.

I recall that my master was not far from believing in this fable of reassuring illusions. Still he didn't think it was *all* illusion. For my part, being younger and less prudent, I was convinced of the opposite. Today I understand our previous attitude better—we didn't want to dismiss religion definitively but we no longer accepted its forms. Before asking if we were right, I want to understand which order we chose to live in since we can't live randomly, after all.

The era in which we had our debates was to my mind stranger than any before it, not in a completely positive or negative way, but in the extent and the number of its contradictions. It was called an 'enlightened' era, freed from ancient fables and yet no other era witnessed more savage crimes, more appalling delirium, more constant or more general terror. The advances in science seemed to open up extraordinary prospects, but on the whole these looked very much like the most naive images of Hell and Paradise. Art, so long subject to the strictest rules, a labour requiring patience and mastery, seemed to be reinventing its first faltering steps as if to better oppose the increasing authority of numbers. Religions lingered on and ran out of breath trying to adapt to rhythms that were essentially foreign to them. Many people were drawn to the surprising allure of the most ancient proofs of human presence and grandeur: leaves of gold buried in the foundations of the palaces of Assur, idols dug up in the Cyclades, words written on clay tablets or on papyrus, temples suspended on mountainsides, springs sheltered by oak trees dedicated to nymphs . . . What was it in these fragments of distant worlds that moved them so deeply? We often spoke of this back then and we had no doubt that this allure had some essential tie both to the light we were following and to the Intangible which my master had come up against, irreparably it seemed. Again, I wonder at this strange change in spirit.

What man had seized upon in these works and in these sites were always precisely human *limits* or, rather, what is past human limits, the absolute beyond, sometimes conceived of as terrifying, sometimes as delightful or both at once. What we could not overlook, therefore, what was imperative for us to consider was that the proximity (if I can put it thus) of the Unapproachable imbued everything created in honour of it or inspired by it with a sort of *magic*, magic that subsisted despite the fact that the cults founded on it had disappeared long ago; magic, after all, and what was not the least surprising was the fact that it seemed never to have been as strong as in our time when everything conspired to draw in human limits, to deny or ignore the Limitless, however it manifested itself. (True, this denial had its advantages: thanks to it, astounding material progress was achieved in all fields. But at what price?) Be that as it may, part of us, deep inside us, clung to this magic as if it showed, in its obscure ambiguity, the way to those who wished to access the best part of themselves. Furthermore, we'd become convinced, if only by measuring the intensity of our emotional reaction to these works and sites to which various religions had attached, each in its own fashion and with varying degrees of clear-sightedness, honesty and rigour, a presentiment of something essential that was nothing more than our bond with that which resists all bonds, our connection with something to which nothing can connect. We'd often remarked to one another at the sight of ancient idols: 'They are more beautiful than others that are nonetheless made with greater knowledge and skill.' And something kept us from admitting that more beauty did not mean more truth. Did the beauty that touched us so deeply it brought us to tears not move us perhaps because it spoke to us of an unforgettable truth, a promise of the only grace that interested us? There was no calculation, no measure, no reasoning that could have justified this hope (its essence and power were no doubt connected to its proving itself unjustifiable and forever questionable). It even appeared ridiculous when compared with events, with evidence (horrifying, increasingly horrifying) of historical events, or even with any extremely simple but inevitable occurrences, like blood flowing from a wound. All the same, more than once we directly experienced other kinds of proof of this hope's existence as well as its unmediated omnipotence and nothing could have prevented that.

Why then didn't we adopt the religion that had survived, the religion of our parents and our entire ancestral stock? Why did we not return to the fold and through our adherence help preserve its fidelity to the sacred, a fidelity that could have been the gauge of a promise kept and the source of a new beauty, a new grandeur? Wasn't that our mistake and the reason my master was so severely punished? And yet, even though we often considered it, we had to admit that we were absolutely incapable of believing everything the Church required of us. We refused to accept that a definitive truth could ever be offered to man, preferring instead to imagine a succession of partial, localized premonitions around which had coalesced everything necessary to create a dogma or system and after a certain number of centuries to smother the flame that had been thought durable. We thought this flame escaped only to reappear continuously elsewhere, always at the risk of turning from a flame into a simple heating source. We also came to think, a bit hastily I'm afraid, that if mankind changes then the Limitless also changes. Some claimed it was gone, others that it had disappeared for now but would return. My master occasionally wondered if, by progressively losing all contours, all countenance, its place in the cities, houses and hearts, all glory and all authority and by disappearing in this way, in coming more and more to resemble absence, distance, an abyss, the Limitless was not showing its essentially ambiguous truth more clearly: the Infinitely Distant, the Imperceptible, the Taciturn. He played with these thoughts, these musings that were somewhat reassuring, even effortless, despite their strangeness: because we were freed from any cult or engagement, from all sacrifice, and a promise was made to us nonetheless (and I now wonder if it were an ease he allowed himself without letting it show or even perhaps without being aware of it). He still believed the powerful and obscure premonitions that had guided him through their uncertainty, even fragility—precisely because they were not part of any existing religion or philosophical system, because they seemed to be floating in the air without ties or justification, without any perceptible guarantee—were, in fact, the last authentic ties that contemporary man had been able to preserve with the Limitless, which had in turn become suspect although beyond doubt, in other words, with the god who, by retreating, sometimes seemed all the greater, more desirable, and nearer than ever.

I won't describe at length the state I was in for the first few weeks following that night. I will only say that if some noise or nightmare woke me from a sound sleep, I experienced a sense of sadness so vast I thought it would never end, and a wave of nausea washed over me. Night, which I knew or, rather, sensed behind the closed shutters, seemed to me to be livid; forced sleep seemed to be the only remedy. Looking around, walking through the streets and especially talking to others took an unfathomable effort.

I couldn't let myself sink like this without defending myself. My master was rather advanced in years and if he hadn't put up much resistance, that was perhaps mostly due to a sense that his life was almost over and his strength gone. Resistance would therefore have been futile. I was still vigorous, having lived barely half of one lifespan. I'd have been a coward to let myself fall into the hole his words dug beneath me. I was less fervent than he had been but more lucid. With my clear-sightedness, I could hope to recover what his passion had not been able to preserve.

It was no easy task—the impetus that drove me was still far inferior to the despair that had overcome me and far more sporadic. It reminded me of the weak light in early spring that shines between long weeks of low clouds, of those tentative warm spells that melt the snow in places, after which it soon falls again, thicker and looking all the colder, the more one thought it would not snow again. I was by no means confident I could overcome, could prevail over this internal winter. My mind, deeply troubled by this completely unforeseen failure, was hesitant. I came up against an infinite number of obstacles when I tried to concentrate on anything whatsoever and therefore couldn't even decide which subjects merited attention. My mind was elusive, as if trying to evade a much too arduous task. It seized upon an image, an unfinished thought, then let it drop for others and finally was left empty, anxious and increasingly sombre. I tried to look at the things around me, things to which I'd become deeply attached once my master had revealed their meaning to me. I'd thought I would never stop cherishing them, imagining instead that as I aged and became more conscious of my mortality, I would appreciate their splendour, value and appeal. And I recalled that he'd once claimed the complete contrary, and to me appalling point of view—that the world does not shine brighter as the end approaches, far from it.

Instead, the imminence of death progressively extinguishes the world, sometimes even quite suddenly, in a single breath, and we can neither prepare ourselves for it nor explain it afterwards. He added that rather than strengthening the connection men feel for the things around them, it loosens or severs them. I felt a sharp sense of distress when I realized these few words had effectively undermined my connection to my surroundings, a connection I'd thought profound. I, too, began to feel the world was *losing its reality*. So perhaps I, too, would become a spectre, someone from far away surrounded by distant things, in truth, a shade floating among shadows and reflections. As a matter of fact, in those earlier years my master had formulated the surprising idea that Dante's *Purgatorio* (a rather cold and naive fiction to the hasty reader), was re-establishing itself on the surface of our world, that our world was being overrun with rootless, suffering, swirling, almost invisible souls lacking even the consolation of the hope that they might work their way up, more or less arduously, towards a shining way out. And if, during those moments of bitter reflection, I turned my attention from the things I saw around me—houses, barges, public squares, gardens—to human events, to history unfolding noisily a bit further off—but not much further off since we saw barricades set up one morning even in my peaceful neighbourhood—then

I could perceive Hell itself close by. If I considered things more seriously, Hell seemed reasonably well-established in the here and there. Yes, all my usual supports, all that had helped and guided me, were slipping away, were being drained of warmth and life. The only thing still near me, still approaching, still almost within reach was ignominy, a horror I refused to explore for fear of becoming complicit with it, however slightly. I had good reason to shudder: I will pass over it quickly. No one needs an account of my ordeal. However, there may be some profit in enumerating the reasons that restored to me, as if in defiance, the taste for battle, the desire to win or at least to resist to my most utmost limit, which I suspected was not very far off.

So I accepted the challenge. I started over, with almost no weapons, my defenses all but powerless: changing faces, half-erased memories, elusive landscapes. And always, my head was filled with the same disarray, the same fog. What's more, each new attempt aged me, and the thought occasionally occurred to me that in pursuing my life, I was using it up—a thought that discouraged me more than any other except for the thought of the end that seemed to be drawing near, to be able to ambush us at any moment. I struggled nonetheless in being unable to fight outright. If I caught sight of a glimmer, I focused all my attention on it. I followed it for an instant. I tried to connect it with others, to gather them into sheaves or bundles. But all I managed to do was scatter them in a new disarray under the same fog. As a last resort I had to adopt a method of cold calculation: just as someone who has lost a ring in the gravel carefully divides the surface into segments and studies them one after the other, I resolved to mark off in sections what I knew of my master's life in order to discover the mistake that cost him so dearly (if, in fact, there was one, and of that I was not at all certain).

My master had rarely spoken of his childhood, unlike many of his kind, by which I mean sensitive, thoughtful men who dive back into their early years with delight. Not that his childhood must have been unhappy, I don't believe it was. Rather, in general, a deep sense of modesty kept him from mentioning his life to others. Besides, as he admitted to me once, he retained very few memories of his childhood and none of them seemed to have anything in common with those of other children. In the end, he found it frightening that so many days should slip into the void even for him who had lived them. (I believe that this is the point on which I can find fault with him. This is perhaps one of the traits that can explain his failure: he did not want to lose, though motivated by fear rather than greed or avarice, he lacked courage . . .). Nonetheless, he would occasionally recall that period on our walks together—we almost always talked while walking so that the distractions presented by the landscape would diffuse the embarrassment of too-serious conversations.

Curiously enough, he was less affected by the loss of his own early years than by the thought of his parents' youth, of what they might have been like when he was only five or six years old. It saddened him that he could barely remember their faces, although they had surely loved him, even spoilt him. From this forgetting, he measured the distance from which children see the adult world, if they see it at all or even care. 'They owned a phonograph and records with passages of famous operas, *Faust*, *La Traviata*, *La Bohême*, as well as popular dance music: foxtrot, slow fox, one-step. They organized balls. They played tennis. Automobiles were still relatively rare and their idea of luxury was a wicker basket specially designed for picnics . . . That, yes, I do recall—that basket which may well have belonged to someone else rather than my parents, more fortunate or more up-to-date friends. It dazzled me. I also remember shivering around fires of glowing embers in autumn on the edges of damp pine forests; witnessing the first attempts at wireless telegraphy, the continual crackling of the station no matter which wavelength the transmission was tuned to, and the constant retuning . . . In retrospect it was a rather easy existence, a happy one, on the whole, but I hardly saw any of it. Trying to reinvent it now would be a melancholy undertaking . . .' Even then, the few times he spoke to me of anything personal because

I'd asked him about it, he seemed to doubt the reality of his childhood and that, more than anything else, kept him from dwelling on his past. He feared that reflecting on his life would put him in a state of horror from which he sensed he might not easily emerge. Indeed, how could he have justified a life so uncertain and elusive? Was it worth living through the present only to lose it past recall? I countered that he could have tried to recapture his life, to preserve it by evoking it, that on his current path he was condemning himself to losing another fragment each year but that he had his own ways of fighting this attrition. He didn't believe me: 'Any effort I make to recover a moment from my past would be subtracted from the present. You see how absurd that would be. Just leave me the bitter satisfaction of knowing that all that survives from that decade in my life are one or two images, frail enough to not weigh on me: the scent of a white peony whose wet petals made my bare legs shiver, the sour taste of rowan berries (and in the pink light of the sunset, in the rowan tree's branches, a swing rises, disappears, reappears), mounted Cossack cavalry officers jumping over a bonfire at night in the Place d'Armes near the train station . . . Rare marvels of a peaceful, protected childhood, filled with little commotion and a happiness I can no longer taste.'

Essentially, I believe he almost automatically turned away from anything that might threaten his security—he'd already sensed that his life might well be nothing more than the whirl of dust motes he mentioned to me later and that if he examined too closely, would be a source of suffering. However, he had no courage at all when faced with suffering, whether of others or his own. For a very long time he was spared—perhaps that's why he didn't resist when suffering did assail him. He only wanted to remember the magic he would try to use later, when the time came, to 'pass over' death. Fire, light, scents. All the same, it was rather strange that among his rare childhood memories (but perhaps he hid quite a few from me?), was one, more vivid than all the others, of a flower's perfume intensified by a rain shower. He had described a similar phenomenon— when you left his little town and entered a small valley often filled with mist from the river that snaked through dense trees, mid-slope, you came upon a canal channelling water to a factory; someone who accompanied him on a walk one day (again, he couldn't remember who it was, his mother, an aunt, one of the servants) had thrown a flower into the canal and the two of them had rushed to follow it on its voyage and watch it be sucked, whirling, into the sluice. 'Do you understand all this? The glow that illuminates this moment in my memory, even forty years on, leads me to believe that it was one of the most beautiful days of my childhood. I find these insignificant things truly poignant when I think about them, and you know that I very rarely dwell on the past happily. It seems that certain moments sink more deeply within us than others and take root, preserving a kind of warmth or radiance even into our advanced age. I can't help but wonder if there's a law that determines the selection of these moments or if it's just a matter of chance. Well! I believe there are reasons and even that they're essential. A scent, the rain, a fire, horses. A canal, a flower, a factory, a humid valley . . . Things in themselves profound, shared experiences that reach the most secret movements and urgent needs of the heart. Things that flee, glitter or dissipate, emanations of Time, apparitions rising from the core of things that pierce the fog of daily indifference, shapes, smiling or serious, in the grip of the Intangible, for lack of a clearer description . . . Do you experience this the way I do?' That is what he said to me one day, the only time that recalling his childhood seemed to animate him, even unsettle him. I understood very well what he meant and I had no doubt he was right. And yet, today, I wonder if he wasn't perhaps too ready to eliminate anything that might bother him, to forget the obstacles and become attached only to favourable evidence, to things that contributed to the clarity of his life; such that when the day came when this evidence disappeared, for whatever reason, when he could not longer rely on it, he was in danger of collapsing, as he then did.

About his love life, he was also surprisingly discreet: nothing was more repugnant to him than the immodesty of modern narratives, the display of private lives, all the squalor and inanities that books and newspapers peddle these days. The truth is, I occasionally asked myself with a touch of malice if his modesty wasn't attributable to the fact that he'd have precious little to tell, or more failures than exploits. Then I discarded that suspicion. He was certainly no conqueror, even if his reputation would have helped in certain circles. After all, I did understand that like most men, he could have told some grand stories of love, often, but not always unhappy. His disdain for confession, his horror of indiscretion were, therefore, real. I appreciated those qualities in a world in which exhibitionism was becoming more pronounced every day, although I did recognize they were also indicative of a lack of generosity, self-abandon and spontaneity. In all respects, I saw that he would have liked to live like a nobleman, a knight—but would he have had the strength? His ambition would have been betrayed by the weakness of his character. He had to keep a tight grip on himself and this strain might have contributed to his collapse.

At the beginning of this account, I described the strange circumstances in which I first met this man who would play such a central role in my life, how I had gone to a reception in his honour, a reception he did not escape from discreetly enough to keep me from following him and how I surprised him in his pursuit of love. Later, after we were bound in friendship, I admitted my indiscretion which, contrary to my expectation, he found touching. He seemed to consider those almost clandestine moments of his youth the happiest, the most real he'd ever known. And surprisingly, he spoke of them gladly. On the topic of this adventure, intimate disclosures didn't bother him at all—precisely because it concerned a completely pure love that was never consummated, not even with a kiss. And so I learnt how the pursuit I'd happened on that night ended, that is to say how the love that only ever burned in his heart was extinguished. I'd often mused about the story of this scene that played out near me without my having any idea because after I'd lost sight of them, I'd lingered on the quay for a long time, down near the river, while they had climbed up to one of the old balconies halfway up the facade of one of the palaces built on its banks. As a result, I saw the same barque that he remembered pass by that night. I looked at the same bright moon. I don't think it bold to recount what I imagined after hearing his story of that night, as if I'd spied on them, which nearly was the case, because even then, struck by the meeting of these two people in a cafe at night, one of whom I knew only from a distance, the other not at all, even then, although having lost sight of them and unsure whether I would ever find either of them again, maybe even because of this, I couldn't keep my thoughts from dwelling on them and, looking now at the stars above me, now at their reflections in the river's surprisingly smooth surface, I pictured the two of them as two successive constellations, fated never to meet. For my part, I named them Actaeon and Diana without caring whether or not the myth applied. I called him Actaeon because I had seen him as avid as a hunter and her Diana because I liked associating her with the moon, with a soft but cold light, with a dweller of the night, a companion of the water. And indeed, while I imagined these two beings who had been little more than two shadows to me, while I pictured them racing across the cool March sky, they were walking above me, but with stops and starts, with doubts that made them much less lofty than the stars, murmuring and stammering blundering words that would have prevented me, had I heard them at the time, from considering them heroes or gods . . .

He held the girl's slender wrist in his hand. For the first time he let show that he didn't want her to leave again as she always did and he was about to tell her this as well; but she, she had backed away slightly so that her arm was extended. She was leaning against the stone doorway, her head slightly tilted towards the river, perhaps looking absent-mindedly at the light of the streetlamps through the branches of the plane trees and the dark water, listening to the almost constant rumble of passing traffic and that voice, too serious, too urgent for her who thought only of acting from morning to night:

'This time, I'm keeping you. I've run too much . . .'

At first she didn't know what to say. She didn't want to stay at all, anyway. She had suspected for a while that the time would come when she would have to stop behaving like a child and speak as adults do, as she herself did on stage, yet this time with repercussions not just in the imagination but also on living people. It would be for her like trying to lift a weight beyond her strength. She smiled and turned her soft, dark eyes from the river to the gallery and the man speaking to her. Her eyes lingered on him only for a moment before turning away again, but she had smiled and tilted her head a bit more, revealing hair of the same shade, the same grace as the darkness. She smiled because it was a tenderness that cost her nothing and she could gauge neither its force nor its cruelty, and because it delayed her response, the phrases she wasn't able to form in her head. As she looked back at the river, she saw a barque sail past, a lit lantern on its bow, following the current with no more noise than an imperceptible breath. She immediately leant over the stone balustrade and, child that she was—forgetting what she'd just been told and the passion of the man who'd been pursuing her for months, forgetting her resolution to finally tell him that she didn't love him, that she didn't want to get married yet and even if she did it would be to someone else—she cried out (he still hadn't let go of her wrist): 'I wish a boat like that would take me away tonight without Mene finding out. I'd like to glide silently between the embankment walls, the shuttered, sleeping houses, then past the factory neighbourhoods you drove me through one day, past brightly lit trains on the viaducts, then past the vast plains . . .'

'And the night turning above you until daybreak . . .'

Then she remembered he was there and in her savagery was irritated that he wanted to intrude on her most cherished daydreams. This gave her the courage to turn to him, at last, and give him more than a glance, perhaps encouraged by the pained longing clear in his face. She spoke very gently as when she wanted to be forgiven for some foolishness or other and this time it was much more than foolishness.

'It wouldn't work, you know that. You've known it since we first saw each other but you're stubborn, and then you'd be unhappy. I've already told you that . . .'

'That's not quite true. Once in a while, maybe without thinking, maybe out of negligence—but I don't believe that—you made me happy and that is a bond between us you can no longer break. When I made that long trip to find you in the horrible country where you have your vacation home, when I spent those many days near you in the garden where we rested like children taking a nap and where we could see the lake glittering behind a screen of reeds, do you remember all that? I told you then—the world around is us a ring that will keep us from ever separating . . . If you didn't believe me, you should have sent me away right then, prevented me from looking at you, from burning every one of your traits, your movements, your looks into my memory (everything, in fact, that he would later be surprised to find he'd almost completely forgotten). I devoured you with my eyes—you know that expression in French—to an extent that you're already a part of me, in a certain sense, a very delicate and tender sense . . . I will keep you and you, in turn, will keep me. I'll help you, you'll see . . .'

He spoke quickly, without leaving any space between his sentences for the girl to slip in any objections or thoughts or bits of her own life. He wanted to envelop her in words and even though he spoke gently and out of what we call love, as if he were trying to capture his prey in a net.

'You know that you're just a child, that Mene won't always be there to protect you and that you'd be lost on your own. Weren't there times when a vast sense of peace spread over us and the most insurmountable difficulties faded in its clarity? We'll recreate it more permanently . . .'

How could he know—since he had never tried to ask—what she experienced during those moments he found so wonderful? Perhaps she was thinking about something else entirely, about the boy she said she loved, or not about love at all but about nothing, about the pleasure of lying in the sun, vaguely aware of being admired, or about desire (although Mene always declared, with the glee of a procuress, that her daughter was completely innocent). He loved her as one loves a dream and dreams are malleable; but it was a dream that was elusive, that dreamt its own dream, so that without being aware of it—he, at least, was not aware—they were always distant from each other, hidden from each other.

'Come closer.'

He tried to pull her towards him, but she slipped away. He saw her run down the long gallery, crossing one after another, bands of shadow and lighted arches, not at all frightened or angry, but smiling, kittenish, waving at him vaguely as her skirt rose and fell with her hurried steps. Then, when he'd caught up with her, a foretaste of misery on his lips, he found her serious again, frowning with the effort of explaining herself, the struggle of finding words that were decisive, but still friendly and kind.

'I want to act for a few more years, not get married so young, as you know, I told you, and that . . . you're not the only one. I'm too silly for you, please listen, I do realize that. There are so many things you say that I don't understand, not at all. Mene tells you often enough that I'm only a child and that if you had to live with me day in day out, you would suffer, you would soon find me unbearable . . .'

'Don't run away again. Walk with me to the end of the gallery.'

The gallery next to where they stood, turned at a right angle along the building's facade, perpendicular to the river, and looked out over a dark narrow street beyond which stood a hotel in the middle of a garden. It was in this garden that the first blackbird song in the village was heard every spring as early as February. From the end of this gallery you could see the park's trees. They were not very high but dense and beyond them the quays and the river were visible, and further off, the sparkle of a public square and hazy clouds of pink smoke crowning the jagged horizon of rooftops. They rested their elbows side by side, facing this view. But the young woman was bored and gradually more and more annoyed with herself for being clumsy and weak, for not mastering feminine wiles and even more for feeling so much affection for this man who had never been anything but respectful and attentive towards her. She sensed it was time to end to this relationship, that later there would be no more excuses for having let him hope, that Mene was working against her and for him. He had begun speaking again, in a voice so low she could hardly hear him.

'Another life . . .'

Caught up again in his old dream, the one I knew so well, he wasn't actually addressing her. It was a kind of private song or thought in a dreamlike state unrolling like smoke, alternatively luminous and black, solitary yet fed by the fire of this presence so near but uncaught. Because he was so close to this supple, childish and sullen person and because she was at the same time still forbidden him, he began to speak differently, to speak contemplatively rather than as a conqueror.

'Another life. It's because we understand the absurdity of ordinary existence that we infer the existence of another—your face reveals it to me. If you weren't constantly turning away from me, as if you were timid, we would enter into that life which is the only true one—it's not another life but the inside of the one men generally lead. The things around us, we won't stop seeing them, but those nearest, like those furthest away, will serve as ramparts, circles of light more or less bright. We will no longer be able to leave these enclosures as long as you keep your face turned towards me. If I've become madly attached to you, it's because I knew, from the very first moment, that you are one of those with whom I can enter the tender core of things and the only one whose rejection will banish me from this core. The others, don't they always seem in a hurry? You'd think they don't find their lives short enough, that they run to end it as quickly as possible. It's that they're removed from the centre where there is no haste, no movement except for that of the surrounding days. You have this power, but without me you wouldn't know it. If you give me your hand, everything will be different for you. But you are more elusive than those summer showers one sometimes sees racing over the fields, barely moistening the ground. But you're afraid of changing because the lazy, the carefree are attached to childhood . . .'

'It's impossible,' she finally plucked up enough courage to say, 'impossible, impossible, impossible. It's all very simple, you see, I'm going to cause you pain, but too bad. I don't want to—I don't give you a single thought, if I even have thoughts, rather than whims and a taste for what I can have right away and a taste for laughter, for dancing. Let me go now, quickly, and forget me completely, think about something else, run just as I'm going to, run far from me, from any memory of me, from any pain you will foolishly suffer on account of my silliness, please, run away from me as from a pointless sorrow, from one of those summer showers you just mentioned, I won't give you my hand, I won't even say goodbye . . .'

Continuing in this vein, she backed away, lowered her eyes and suddenly fled. She ran without stopping. The lightness of her steps was more wrenching for my master than her words had been. He stood without moving, his back to the garden and the cold he felt rising from the river and the streets. He waited for at least one last graceful wave of her hand before she descended the steps to the level of the quays and returned, in just a few minutes, to Mene's. Yet if she did turn back, he couldn't have seen it because the night had grown much too dark.

In this scene, I recognized a story as old as the world, 'the millionth love story' as my master would later say bitterly, seeing in the phase of his life he'd so long considered happy only the distressing repetition of a chronic mistake. (In the meantime, he must have preferred the serenity and richness of his life in the country.) Wasn't it strange, all the same, this fever sparked or, rather, fixed by a face he hadn't chosen at all? Since adolescence, perhaps also since childhood, though more vaguely, an impulse had driven him, as with many of us, towards a presentiment of a higher, more ardent life than the one he saw reflected around him, a desire for something he couldn't name and which wasn't necessarily tied to someone living. His walks through splendid autumn landscapes, his reading, his dreams, his early travels (which he'd admitted to me he did foolishly, seeing everything through a fog of anxiety and sadness, 'an idiot, a complete idiot, that's what I was at twenty'), in short, everything he accomplished that was not done out of duty, these were steps he took towards this unknown thing he didn't know where to seek. His adolescence, he said, was nothing more than a long sleep punctuated by apparitions, some of them overwhelming. Maybe the girls he'd loved back then were precisely the faces or bodies emerging from this sleep to which the majority of other people had no access? But why this one rather than another? In response to this confused ardour, he must have composed a face in his mind that incarnated this very ardour. When he saw certain traits in a woman passing by, he immediately forgot other traits that perhaps didn't correspond closely to his model, so great was his joy to see his dream confirmed in reality, to feel it so close, tangible and graceful.

What was it he had loved in the young foreign actress if not, as he himself had recognized, that intact youth and an extremely distant grace? He wasn't actually concerned with loving her even though he believed he loved her passionately, deeply enough to sacrifice his sense of self, his reputation, his immediate needs. What I mean is that he didn't want to know her deeply, to help her flower freely, to listen to her, to know who she was—that surely never occurred to him. Some part of him had decided, independent of his will or thought, that she would be the light that would lead him out of the unhappy darkness in which he had wandered for too long. Saying that she was for him like the moon, soft, cold, distant, passing over the village roofs, obscured now and again by pylons and towers, is not to put things poetically. If he had drawn too close to her, if she had let him, he would soon have seen her brilliance fade whereas, in fact, if I can believe what he told me, it was on the night she definitively dismissed him that his love blinded him most intensely. This then was the light of dreams, of absence, of refusal, but also of the possible. The young woman's flight woke him from a torpor into which he didn't realize how deeply he'd sunk. The pain he suffered sharpened his mind, deepened his attention to the world around him, kindled his pride. He had the illusion of resembling the legendary tragic heroes and his pain soon turned into a severe, melancholy happiness. He who had floated for so long between two worlds believed he was finally living because he was suffering and he rejoiced in his suffering. He was filled with an extraordinary energy. The more days passed, the more he felt able to rise above other men. Did he ever think of the girl to whom he owed this intoxication, did he worry about her at all? Less and less, I'm afraid. Fortunately for him, she maintained exactly the right distance between them, any less and she would simply have been prey soon abandoned. The tension created by precisely this distance was necessary for their relationship to engender clarity and strength within him. Then she became too distant; he didn't think of following her elsewhere and he never knew what became of her.

This love, this strange and yet so common kind of love in which the beloved is loved only insofar as he or she is not known, held, possessed, in which a certain distance is maintained, was essentially idolatry, the unconscious return to that old dream of escaping the world and time. The girl had been chosen at the moment when she could play the role of a divinity, in which no separation between her and Diana was perceptible (so that he always pictured her running ahead of him between trees on clear nights). She had achieved that perfection we wish unchangeable. She embodied a grace that is impossible to maintain, that changes if one draws near. Was it a lie then, a mistake? One could surely say that love is wanting to steal what we love away from time and also the need to flee the object of our love in order to be illuminated by it. And it certainly is strange to allow one's life to depend on a face one has glimpsed, to declare one loves only that face and would die if separated from it, especially with little concern for the person behind it and the fact that this person also has a life and interests . . . Nevertheless, this blind love—awkward and awed—was not merely the height of egotism and an illusory happiness. A sign was hidden in its impetus—this blaze did not burn completely in vain or by chance.

Before his downfall and despite his tendency to smile at the raptures of the young, my master found it unthinkable that so much passion in so many people dissipated into pure unreality. Indeed, he admitted one must accept time, that true love should include it (a difficult feat which he would not manage to do), and yet, to disregard this age-old dream, to see in it only a long and ultimately sinister mistake seemed to him another and more serious form of delusion. This powerful impetus—irresistible, unthinking, uncalculated—was necessary as was the disorderly movement of his pursuit for a man to remember later, once he has been disabused of his belief that he has prevailed and possessed, that life cannot be reduced to a series of transactions, for him to recognize he is constrained to hold in his hands both the dream and the things of the earth or he will risk annihilation. The memory of this folly was necessary to keep my master from turning the wisdom he believed he'd attained into a possession and making of it a fire able to burn away any temptation towards abasement. Dreams, the clarity in which a young woman had bathed the world for moment, the spirit's brief illuminations in transports of love, the hum of words tossed into the air for nothing, for the simple pleasure of hearing them rise like birds then move on, leaving behind a wider, more limpid sky, nights in which all of life had seemed to gather into eyes suddenly filled with tenderness and fear, all those moments open to a more noble future, bonds revealed between realities, each of which, when taken in isolation, seemed elusive and empty, all of this—even though later, his spirit wounded, he would declare it all misleading or extremely doubtful—all of this cannot be arbitrarily erased from human experience. This was the evasive, intangible aspect of human existence, never grasped, never possessed, never definitively named—it was perhaps its most necessary sustenance, the magic root heroes had sought in the remotest corners of the earth in times past and for which they'd undergone dreadful challenges. But you could say that nothing in a man's life is as precarious and as difficult to preserve, because the very desire to preserve it puts it more surely at risk . . . Not only each particular lifespan, each day severed from the future by time's sharp hatchet assaults this elusive aspect, but also the movement of centuries. Perhaps soon, my master would say when overcome with discouragement, there won't be any more first loves— men will be too brutish or too wise, animals or machines. Haven't we already witnessed, during a recent war, almost an entire people incorporate the ferocity of beasts and the efficient precision of machines to a terrifying extent? Thus we know in advance the possible cost of rejecting uncertainty.

I don't want to tell my master's life story, out of respect for his discretion and mostly because there is not enough time. I write these lines in order to bring clarity to places in which I am lost, in order to find my way out more quickly, not to linger on ancient stories and, above all, not to brood over the bitterness of regret. I would like to finish quickly—there's no enjoyment holding me back. I've spent enough time on these questions, I've put off examining them long enough. I must be resolute and then, without delay, leave this mess behind me. Something urges me on—a desire for lightness before it's too late, a calling from the air as if there were, at the end of this book, an open, happy space, an imminence of light. However, attaining it presupposes some groping in the dark.

What bothered me most, I believe, was suddenly finding my master in the condition I've described after having left him in a state of great serenity. I might have been less surprised if I'd been living near him and his family and if I'd watched the transformation occur (though I have no idea if it was gradual or sudden). My work required me to live on another continent for several years. During that period we only exchanged a few, very banal letters. It was he, after all, who insisted that I live this new phase of my life on my own, having no doubt decided that his teachings should be followed by the test of solitude. I had left a man whom, on reflection, I could only picture as radiant, at peace, sure of himself; and I found, with no warning—as if the three-year interval counted for nothing—the man I described at the beginning of this account, an unhappy man, like so many others, a being shrivelled by the thought of death like a plant that has been placed too close to the fire.

At this point I should return to those months in which I lived with them (because he had brought his wife with him and this woman had borne him a son) in the countryside where he had sought refuge from the growing clamour that surrounded his name. All who saw them at the time were struck, not by the splendour of their lives, because their life together was not splendid—it had its dull moments and difficult passages and lacked a certain amount of cheer and was rarely carefree—but by the sense of peace that seemed to surround them. They didn't have that fierce, harried look people have today. In the village where they'd chosen to live, they were appreciated for exactly that, because they demanded little, even allowed others to take advantage of them, if it came to that, without feeling it necessary to make a fuss over some merchant's petty trick. When I think back on those days (which I find difficult because it always calls up the sight of the foundering shadow who spoke to me that night, and associating the two pictures of him is distressing), when I can bring myself to recall those days and block out how they ended, in other words, when I can recall those days as I saw them at the time and how my master and his wife seemed to live them, I immediately feel that there is more air around me, an immense space. I forget the city whose din assaults me now and I hear the wind whistle through this space and the wind isn't just the steady noise of factories, this tireless force, but a light, because it does, in fact, change the light; when it blows, the entire countryside seems to shimmer like a silver-coloured sea rather than a blue or golden one. I find myself brought back all of a sudden, all at once, into that animated, vigorous air—how many walks we took then!—into that world shining like a mirror and full of revelations.

I've already said that I don't want to get stuck in the past; yet, I must not imitate my master in this. I have to overcome this scruple, because if I can't accept a return to the past, my path will remain obscure.

For him, the time when he vainly pursued a carefree girl was over, as was the more miserable time when, in utter loneliness, he was grovelling at some bitch's feet although she would no doubt have preferred he either slap her or shower her with gold. What was it then? Shall we say it was the marvellous world that appeared to him when he loved the young actress, a dream she could not understand but which had taken on an incredible intensity for him? Can I put it like that? Is there a place in such a world for arguments, for a crying child, a shopkeeper's ledger? And how could a man who is not in on the heart's secret answer that question? As for me, I was profoundly happy in their company—won over by their serenity, I did not doubt that each day would be a promise kept. I was ready to conquer the future.

My master never mentioned his companion in our talks. He was more discreet towards her than he had been towards his first love. Only once he said to me: 'To whom do you think I owe this new heart that is elated by the sight of a simple blade of grass? If I praise a flower or a field, I am actually singing her praises—is there any need to point this out?' And so I had the sense that two beings had joined together, if not to live the *other life* every instant, then at least to never forget it. For my part, if I depict those days, perhaps that will be enough to give a sense of how happy they were.

They had invited me to spend the months of September and October with them. I would have my own room and would not feel I was a burden in any way . . . I didn't hesitate for long.

I usually spent the mornings in my room, working, reading or daydreaming—occasionally my master would come find me. From the beginning he told me: 'You're wrong to place your desk so far from the window. Do you think you'll work better if you keep your back to this? Let's put it up front, instead. Each of our acts, every one of our works should be nothing more than the blossoming of our daily view.' At the time I was like many young people—I lived a waking dream, a strange reflecting fog that I took for the beauty of life but it was just the presentiment of it. My master had opened my eyes. He showed me things, but in such a clear, limpid way that I had the impression I would be able to discover them all after him. And so I began watching the days pass over the hillsides and the distant mountains, as well as over the small street under my window. I did not, strictly speaking, observe; if I looked too long or too closely, I felt I was draining the view of its truth. Instead, I cast furtive, greedy glances and each time I was surprised. I would hear the sounds of their lives in the house and in the garden, sounds that to my ears rang as clear as the plashing of a fountain. Their boy, still too young for school, spent his days in the garden with other children. I'd have never imagined that anyone could play so seriously and then be as flitting and agile as a sparrow. Sometimes, when I no longer heard their shouts or the creaking of their bicycles, I would lean out of the window to make sure they weren't up to any nonsense. I would see them, three or four little boys, standing under a tree talking in low voices with great animation and a passion, a gravity so happy, so candid and especially so carefree, it would fill me with both intense happiness and deep sadness—because of what I dreaded would happen to them later. Then, in an instant, they passed from their almost-solemn immobility to wild leaps that brought my friend to his window with threats of severe punishment. They calmed down and, grumbling, milled around for a few minutes, one, his head lowered, drawing circles in the dirt with the tip of his wooden sword, another tearing a leaf off a bush and chewing it in a rage. Then again, as if they were in cahoots with the wind that in that region never lets anything rest, they threw themselves into a new game, forgetting their pique. My master's companion appeared in turn, blinded by the bright sunlight, her arms filled with wet laundry and raising her tender smile towards our windows, protested that she'd never finish her chore. Her cheerful complaints were then drowned out by a chainsaw starting up, invisible, under the linden trees by the side of a road further down. These were the sounds, alternating between soft and strident, that announced the end of summer even though the colour of the leaves hadn't yet changed. What had changed was the air. On some rare days, when clouds hid the sun, we felt the first hints of cold like frozen columns marching across the fields even in the middle of the heat, after which a temperature set in that was both cool and warm, light and brisk, along with a transparent light. The sky was almost no longer blue and a golden dust lay under the trees. Mornings, when I looked out of my window—now that I had moved my desk in the fear of abandoning all serious work, of finding all the books I could or would want to read unnecessarily complicated, verbose, obscure—I saw at first, because the view was very extensive, the earth awaken, take form in a successive layers of haze, circles or banks of fog. Yet the fog was dazzling: something floated in the light, a harmony of clouds and golden smoke. Now I could almost say, if I weren't afraid of altering the simplicity of it all, that it was an exhalation of incense, something celestial, a movement of light in the very heart of light. Then a mountain, a copse of trees, the imperceptible bend of a river gradually appeared as they woke, and later, even though the sun blazed brighter as it rose, even though this vague enchantment had given way to signs of midday, the wind preserved the scintillation, the animation that, more than anything in the world, gave me a taste for life, a need to live and filled me with boundless energy. Well! Wasn't this the *other life*, the incredible attraction of which my master had tried to make the young Russian woman feel? It was the life of every person, but with everything in it bathed in a light that seemed to me to be closest to divine light, including scoldings, sorrows, arguments; despite appearances, all of it suspended in the air's transparency . . .

Towards evening, we would take walks together —the little boy and I often ran ahead, leaving behind the parents side by side and almost always silent. This was another kind of magic we were allowed to witness. But again, there's no reason to believe we were advancing before it like fanatics preceding their god. We were simply out for a walk, sometimes weary or dully irritated, but usually ready to laugh and not very different from the child who accompanied us. We had not set out to worship a pagan divinity. Insofar, at least, as I can interpret my friends' emotion, which seemed in unison with mine, it was simply the case that we were once again, without even thinking, bathed by the outdoors, and the outdoors was above all the air, the light, moments of night and day. At the hour we liked to walk, the sun had set only a few moments before. Along our path—a path that skirted what can't be called a small valley but, rather, a slight depression, a wide, damp, shallow hollow, divided into vegetable gardens, fields and prairies bordered by willows and poplars above which the last swallows wheeled—along our path the naked earth, collapsed here and there to reveal the twisting roots of oaks, and the rock seemed to keep the day trapped within, while everywhere else, except in the sky's expanse, shadow seemed to be making off with it. This dirt, these sections of almost yellow dirt that rose to our left as we headed out, on the elevated side of the hollow that formed a wooded hillside at the top of which began an arid, windy plateau (and Venus approached us through the black leaves), these sections of dirt or rock outcrops were surrounded by dark garlands of ivy and—how can I say it—we had the impression that light was internal to them as if in a lamp or a fire, but that doesn't quite capture it and I don't know if I will ever find the words to express what it meant in our eyes. Maybe I should say that these sections, because their luminosity was wreathed in dark ornaments, reminded us of small monuments at the feet of which moreover one might find a flower as offering, nourished by the water that seeped around their bases. As a result, we felt we were walking through a peaceful funerary alley in which stone lanterns remained dully lit in memory of ancient warriors, of dead shades or, simply, of the day.

Perhaps, indeed, it was a more modest feeling and, indeed, stranger, more difficult to grasp, this taciturn happiness at a suspension of time. It appeared in our midst unexpectedly, like an unknown woman so beautiful we couldn't look at her without tears, before feeling the slightest twinge of desire or thinking the most fleeting thought. It was, in any case, another trick of the light, one of its mysterious gifts. Maybe we were moved at the sight of the barest earth, the dust, the harsh rock turning into a silk lantern while frail things—the leaves, the grass—already belonged to the night. On the other hand, might it not have been tied to the sun's disappearance, to how deep the movements of day and night, as well as of the seasons sink within us? Not all the light, then, was departing. Its gentleness, its warmth, its company remained here and there as if to guide us: the final fragments, the final hours of the day whereas the day seemed finished. Above all, perhaps, a light whose source had until then not only been visible but also sovereign, almost insolent, so that it was obvious this light gilded what it touched. Now that its source was more invisible than an actual source under the trees, it seemed to emanate from inside the earth, from the heart of the rock. 'Marvellous moments between two worlds, between two times,' my master would say, 'in which being near extinction, under threat, near death, light collects itself inside things, making these final moments the sweetest, the most profound, the dearest to our hearts. And so we walk, lit from within by a light all the more intimate, the closer it is to being extinguished . . .'

How he would later forget those words, even those steps! And yet how true they seemed when he spoke them on our return from one of those walks at the close of day, speaking in a low voice as he watched his wife play with their child in the shadows, at that point almost entirely black, from which the clear sounds of the night rose like stars! In such moments, was there already the slightest break in his voice that could have presaged, for an ear more attentive or more practised than mine, the dark stammering in which his hoarsened voice would eventually exhaust itself? No doubt I was young, that is to say, distracted, and was not on the lookout for such signs, so happy to experience such hours that it didn't occur to me to wonder if they would ever end or if they masked anything less peaceful, less perfect. And surely I'm now obligated to admit that I might have been less than clearsighted. Or did the rupture, in fact, happen abruptly, like a sudden fall from abundance into the void? Be that as it may, I can't help but paint those days as happy ones but, once again, filled with a superior kind of happiness, not at all what I expected. My hosts performed no extraordinary feats. At first sight, the banality of most of their actions might have disappointed. They were not at all insouciant, nor privileged in the usual sense of the word. There was simply that unexpected clarity in the air that struck me at once and illuminated, or seemed to illuminate, their very thoughts.

And so the days passed with the lightness of birds and their flight, their swiftness was another aspect that made them shine. As one looks at a river that sparkles in the distance as far as the eye can follow it, I had no reason to think that time would also shine as far the eye could see. True, we were not immobile, we changed because we were alive; but our course drew a light and a song from us, as from an arrow in flight, and even if we didn't ask to change we agreed to run (and let us not forget that this is an image to translate the invisible because we were also all charged with modest, but difficult work). I believe it was the tireless wind that inspired us to imitate it, that carried us on its noisy wing. I wonder if by dint of seeing the wind, the wind and the light, change the mountains into vapours, we didn't end up seeing all obstacles melt away. We flew without forgetting that our flight would end, but this end—it was my master who said this and how, after all, could I forget words of such clarity, such boldness coming from one who was naturally prone to prudence and worry?—this end was also the motor of our flight.

He thus almost completely reversed the terms. He saw in death the primary nutriment of life, in absolute darkness he saw the flame, in this target, strangely, he saw the very force that bent the bow. It was a kind of mad dream, I'm beginning to realize now that I've seen the consequences—affliction upon affliction. Nonetheless, I did experience those moments, we experienced those moments when the end of our course was, in a sense, flooded with light, as if our arrow were headed straight towards a con-flagration, towards the centre of the sun. And the day's hours followed one after the other, like a pro-cession of present moments even when—or perhaps especially when—we paid no attention, when we were busy with other things. I would stand at my window to wave to the child, to offer my help and, turning to face the west (it was once again evening), I noticed that large, damp hollow where we so often walked and the prairies turn dark green, almost black (while the sky along the horizon turned yellow again, then silver) in a perfectly calm pattern of meadows alternating with cultivated fields; again I would be overcome, as if a bit of grass at a certain hour could appear or, rather, remain hidden but call us nonetheless, as some secret in our own lives. Was this still part of the dream we three cherished and must I one day call this dream, as my master mut-tered, our *blindness*? I remember these moments, I

remember them with intensity. And now that I've
seen the one to whom I owe these moments almost
dead—as good as dead—and in despair and now
that I know he abandoned those whom he deeply
loved and who—I haven't the slightest doubt—were
the source of his happiness, well, the horror I witnessed is not enough to erase or alter what I experienced, absorbed, savoured. It was not such moments
that failed him. It was he who was unfaithful to them,
who betrayed or perhaps sullied them. The more I
sink into them—I can't keep from doing so—the
more valuable they are in my eyes, the more violent
the rage that fills me against the man who wanted to
wrench them away after having offered them to me
and who switched—I still don't understand why—
to the camp of his old enemies, men I still consider
my enemies.

How is it that in this deepening, this darkening of the
greenery, this simple meadow at a certain hour of day
when, in contrast, the sky grew lighter, turning a
shade of silver, there was a call, a murmur that rose
perhaps from the depths of long years? All the same
it could have been any number of things, shade, grass
under the trees, things completely foreign to my life,
of course (I was not so foolish as to think otherwise).
It was just a moment in the day, a fragment of the
world ... How could I not find some relation between

them and human love, our blood, our bones, our skin with their moods, their movements, the heat and cold that runs through them in turn? I didn't ask myself these questions at the time—my emotions left them no room. It's only now, albeit weakened by what I had to witness, that I'm trying to establish these presentiments (and yet don't those who try to prolong a flash betray its nature?). I experienced those moments and was enriched by them and now that they seem less close, I feel the need to fix them, scattered as they are, to collect them, to make them my own. This is probably something I shouldn't do, something that will hasten their ruin. And isn't this the way my master was lost? Still, on the other hand, wouldn't it be trickery to refuse to follow that intimate movement that drives us to question and to understand? Was I not coming up against an insurmountable obstacle in this endeavour?

At some point in his life (but when exactly did this moment occur and what caused it?), my master must have left the circle whose enchantment I've been trying to describe in these pages. And so, just as I've begun to do, from then on he saw the happiness in which he'd previously been immersed only from the outside. He could look as much as he liked, with longing or infinite regret, the more he looked, the farther from his reach it would be. Yes, I believe I can detect in this a kind of cruel game, the meaning of which I still don't understand—the light is not given to those who seek it (the Scriptures also tell us this), it is cruelly withdrawn from those who have known it, but were unable to stay in its purview . . .

Is it then the case that we are unable to remain faithful to it? Because when I had spoken with my master earlier about a possible separation from the light, he had reassured me, saying that what was essential was not to betray its memory, should we think we had lost it, therefore, to remain faithful like someone waiting for dawn, of whom we can believe that it is precisely his waiting for dawn that will make the end of night possible.

Was this not an oversimplification on his part, a display of excessive confidence? I've already mentioned his penchant for simply forgetting whatever bothered him in his life and in his thought. Wasn't he putting too much emphasis on this? He obviously sensed the fragility of his happiness (more than I did); still, *in order to avoid suffering*, he had convinced himself that, should he lose this happiness, it would be sufficient for him to preserve the memory and taste of this happiness inside him over the course of the ordeal that would follow. In this way, he could survive the ordeal without harm . . . But what is an ordeal without harm?

It seems to me, and this is why I'm suspending my reflections for a moment, that at this point I'm close to discovering at least one of the reasons for his collapse: he talked of ordeals, but since he spoke as if he'd overcome them in advance, they were no longer ordeals. He could not or would not acknowledge that the ordeal consisted precisely of being incapable of remaining faithful, of seeing the former abundance as if surrounded by an unscalable wall, such that he would loathe the very sight of it. The more ethereal, brilliant, transparent a land is, the more the sight of it must be difficult for those who have been expelled from it. Hounded from that point on by a memory suddenly turned ironic, by that now-ferocious splendour, he must have sought refuge in the darkest of dark cities and the words I had heard him say were the ashes this newly bereaved man did not tire of putting on his head.

I am suddenly overcome with a sense of immeasurable loss, of hopeless ruin: my master has died long before his physical death, which may still not have come at this point. It distresses me to think he could have been laid so low and to have seen him in his humiliation. This stretch of grass, almost black at dusk, that spoke to me mysteriously and whose words, although obscure, seemed infinitely reassuring—did it lie to me? I could not pull my eyes away. The sky, as clarity fled ever higher in the heavens, seemed nothing more than a passage towards lightness, it seemed to be a wing turning from dark blue to silver while, below, this patch of grass seemed to open up and sink towards the depths and to bring me back to ancient things through thick layers of time. As a result, at that moment, I had the sensation—without understanding it immediately—of being pulled between the heights and the depths like a figure of enormous dimensions and perhaps also extending between past and future, as well as between vaguely sad memory and exalted dream. I could see that a thought, if not a funereal apprehension, contributed to this spreading shadow and, surprisingly, this apprehension filled me with a kind of joy, very deep and very intense . . . I imagined the shadow telling me, 'Thus do I conquer and dig and move things along, such is each phase of your life, such will be your death and for a part of you there will be no ruptures, just as each hour is succeeded by the next . . . Live at peace in what is barely a house of leaves, barely an encampment of darkness, live happily through this passage, you whose tears have always associated you with the transparency of water . . .'

I thought then that there were three of us listening to such counsel and listening only to it. The child never went to bed without provoking a whirlwind of laughter and protest, chases from top to bottom of the house, then we would hear him talking or singing to himself in bed. And suddenly, peace would descend; the wind died with the night.

Those days, those months, were they simply a suspension of time? Is that all they could ever be? Did their lives later eventually come to resemble all other lives again, finally undone by fatigue? And yet, as I've said before, there was nothing exceptional about their lives and so there is no obvious reason why they shouldn't have continued on as they were. Just because the two of them were going to grow old? Just because of time's passage, as my master had foreseen? Still, based on what I could judge from the outside, they weren't bound by passion, those two. They seemed, rather, like two friends, two close companions, neither unduly impressed by the other and, despite what appeared some days to be a certain coldness between them, I had the impression that they were in league with each other, profoundly so, and that no tragedy could divide them. In any case, even though they spoke little, I noticed that they could not bear to be apart for long. I wonder now, however, if I haven't been a mediocre witness on this point. Maybe I should have tried to see things not just through my master's eyes but also through his companion's. I wonder if, even at the time, things would have appeared as clear. Maybe it was her beauty, her youth, that impelled him, that launched his pronouncements like feathered arrows, maybe she shone on his life like the moon? I have no idea, on the other hand, whether what he offered her in return was probably not exactly what she expected? Will I have to condemn the one I admired so deeply for no other reason than to safeguard my hope, my life's future? How suspect my condemnation will be from then on, if I ever manage to express it! But if I leave all these questions unanswered, they will weigh me down, I will never be free of them. All I need to know is if the tragedy could have been avoided or if it was fated to be; in other words, if that lucid man was destined to collapse.

For months now, my spirit has been feeding two groups of contrasting images that I would like to believe belong to two separate stories that have been confused: images of my master surrounded by his own, often obviously preoccupied but with that quasi-certainty that all difficulties can be overcome and, above all, with that tranquillity, those smiles, signs of patience, joy and tenderness, that moderation, so surprising in a world where it is usually confused with mediocrity; and the images of the endless night in which I found him like the 'Justly Punished', taking up the eternal lamentation of those we have too quickly judged vain and called repugnant.

Abandoning this book is something I've wanted to do more than once since I began it. Tired of drifting between elusive thoughts and unable to put them in any order, how often the prospect of burning these pages seemed a relief!

History only too often confirmed my unhappy master's words—the reasons for rejecting the world stared me in the face. In one sense, his position was the stronger one, he was better armed with arguments and the consequences he drew were logical and simple, almost too simple. If *nothing was*, then it was better to commit suicide than play the game. The time had come for this terrible truth and our final grandeur would be to stop disguising it . . .

And yet, other minds had drawn strength from this same confrontation, concluding that the Invisible was merely a flaw in our vision or that it does exist, but beyond our world. They fearlessly decided to exhaust the possible and their lives were occasionally revealed to be full of clarity and power. I admired the pride in these men whose almost confident belief in nothingness stoked their desire to act, to love, to conquer. I'd met several such men, especially during my years abroad in a country more resolutely turned towards the future for not being weighed down as we are by treasures from a long history. They had surprised me with their health, their mettle, their vigour. I would have like to see in them the best surety for human hope. Their ventures were not logically justifiable since they didn't believe them safe from eventual ruin, but the bitter happiness that drove them gave their relentlessness an altogether different justification, perhaps sufficient . . .

And yet, I'd never sincerely wished to join them. Even in the bleakest days that followed the meeting with my master, I didn't consider it. In spite of it all, something else continued to speak deep within me. I soon had an odd surprise.

The solemn gravity of my statements annoyed me: Where had I found this tone? Didn't I realize it diverted me from the truth? Did I think I was writing a treatise, composing a sermon? A fierce impatience rose in me against these words so quick to combine into harmonious phrases, into waves of eloquence. I thought it was the world, the truth of the world, stronger than all ruin, that had returned to shove aside my wisdom, my gravity. I wished a great laugh would scatter questions and answers, doubts and hypotheses, the entire meticulous but fragile construction. I was suddenly in a rush, a rush to live, to reject my master's example, in a rush to assert my youth which had not succumbed.

Would I much longer call *dream* what was best and clearest in our lives and *reality* a weakness of that heart attached to foolish, tangible guarantees? Pursued for a while by soft, cunning voices, I felt them now being chased away by others, much calmer and firmer, if not louder. Was it really necessary to know where they came from and where they would lead me if their tone contained the decisive force of life?

My master . . . I would have liked to keep his memory free from all injury, but not at the cost of my future. Besides, this wasn't a matter of putting him on trial. But when I mentioned his constant fear of losing, when I evoked his unhealthy terror of death or even suffering, I touched on the real explanation of his fall. His brilliance was surely in large part attributable to his obvious qualities, but also to chance—he had been well protected . . .

I first met him when he was fleeing fame in pursuit of a marvellous love and I found him later, again in flight to protect another love. I'd admired a man who refused the coming glory that seemed perfectly justified. And yet, wasn't it in him merely a more subtle form of pride? It was not difficult for him to refuse the fame of salons that flatters only lowly souls; and he must have been well aware that in refusing it, he would be assured another, purer kind of fame, the pleasures of which he would peacefully cultivate in his garden, gathering in both happiness and integrity.

A devil of a man! So modest, seemingly so detached—still, didn't he try to have it all? Fame without compromise, love without its risks, unhappiness without its poison, the visible and the invisible, time and ecstasy outside of time? And I saw him stamp his feet like a spoilt child at the first refusal . . .

I didn't think of claiming, as a result, that he had been a calculating man or even a hypocrite putting on a front of purity, of humility, to ensure tangible gains. Still, didn't he fall, semi-consciously, into the numerous traps that are set for us in all directions, traps that even saints were not always able to avoid? He could nonetheless rightly consider himself less impure, less vile than most other men. The truth for him, I told myself as if it were my own truth, would have been to withdraw completely. Had he ever forgotten himself? His wife, his child, and I myself, though less so, only served to keep him from the void, and the beauty of the world enveloped him more than it fed him. What was it then that he'd suppressed—certainly not his life, but his interest in his own life? Had he been reduced to nothing at all, he would have regained everything!

In this period of impatience, which happened to coincide with a marvellous urban spring, the turbulence of the river, the buzzing of the trees, I suddenly remembered what happened to me in my master's house at the end of a night during which the uncertainty of youth had kept me awake. The shutters were closed but, being dilapidated, they let a little morning light filter into the room, and this light, perhaps because of my fatigue and my passing sadness, seemed to be livid. Hideous bird cries rang out. If I'd kept the shutters closed, I would have felt like a prisoner in limbo, condemned to wander for eternity through a land filled with moaning and fog that seemed the very picture of life. But I finally got up, shivering, and when I pushed open the shutters that creaked like heavy doors, what I saw at first glance were the birds I'd heard crying with such ferocity or despair. Swifts wheeled very fast and very high in the air above me and the air itself seemed limitless, open on all sides, lighter, higher, clearer than ever before. I didn't stop to wonder if these birds lived in a vertigo of elation or if they were bound by inexorable laws, as is most likely. Nor did I wonder if the joy the sight of this dawn inspired in me were necessarily more convincing than the sadness I'd felt on hearing the birds' sharp cries and seeing the grey filtered light. It had nothing to do with that, I felt it quite clearly even though I didn't understand it. I'd simply witnessed one of those scenes that can exhilarate me for days or weeks. Like a swimmer touching ground, I had found my footing again—some might say I was walking on visions. Why not? I no longer cared if others approved of me or ridiculed me. From this point on, my maturity would consist of being less timid, less hesitant. Nothing but flashes of light could answer all questions.

I forgot my sorrow. I thought I'd won because I'd regained my insouciance. A long time passed before I understood, until the day when I no longer simply had to consider the sorrows of others but had to experience my own. And once again, everything teetered on the edge of the void.

It was easy for me to claim victory, I who had never yet been wounded by the breath of time—these words, always these words that flow and are never stopped . . . I'd done little more than follow my master's course, hardly modified, and having not yet reached the icy regions, nothing seemed easier than denouncing the weakness that, in my view, had stranded him there. When I ended up there myself, my pride fell and if I'm there still, to bring this account to an end, my confidence is of another kind.

It's easy to withdraw when happiness carries us. We praise the world, we note its splendour because we're aligned with it. It's the unhappy who talk incessantly of themselves. Suffering closes their eyes, clouds their vision. Withdrawing when we feel bruised or, more simply but no less painfully, empty, cut off from everything we loved most, deprived even of love, wanting only to end one's existence, or deprived even of this last desire, almost dead, in other words, this is what he was able to do, an almost impossible feat. I understand it now. I could not understand from the outside. I don't need to recount my own ordeal, the course of my life, explain who I am. (At most, if I did not succumb like my master, it is probably because I was less sensitive and I hadn't reached the same heights.)

Now it's enough for me to say that if there is a real life, if the reflections we've glimpsed aren't deceptive, we are never allowed to believe ourselves the final inhabitants, to settle in, nor, in the belief we've defined it, to invite others in. All speech tends to delimit something that wants to be defined and will perish from being defined. Therefore, we can neither keep silent nor speak without constantly correcting ourselves. There is one thing we have an irrepressible desire to express and which we must not say. That's why our task will never cease before death.

Carried by fame, by an unhappy love, then by a happy one, my master lived for a long time like the birds that resemble fleet gods, destined to become as one with the eternal light or with those snows at such high altitude they never stop gleaming. Such was the shape the old divine dream took in him. He thought he knew suffering because he saw it from above, just as the inhabitants of the skies can formulate an idea of our walls and our traps. When he met suffering head on, it seemed to him at first as merely an obstacle to be overcome, beyond which, provided he could clear it, he'd find the old happiness intact but as something which, not content to stop the heart's expansion, casts doubt on whether or not that heart had ever soared. He must have seen in suffering not, as he'd always believed, an enemy who could be fought and defeated, rather like night confronts day, but a conqueror nothing can resist, a night that would obliterate even the memory of day or the longing for it. Suffering left him only the fear of destroying himself in it in order to finish a struggle that was not only unequal, but completely pointless.

I can no longer make the claims I made with overtones of impatience and defiance when I thought I'd understood my master's error. You might think I, too, am on a path to destruction, but that's not at all the case. Still, how can I express what lives only off uncertainty and contradiction? At a certain point, my master hit an impassable limit. He who dreamt only of passages couldn't accept this impediment. I, on the contrary, believe that everything starts with this impediment, and before life comes up against this refusal it is but a fragile dream, and only after the refusal does it become an indestructible peril. It's true, therefore, in one sense, that I lost all confidence, having abandoned my belief that the privilege of a supposedly pure glance would guide my steps to the divine abode without fail. And yet, full of doubt, divided, more devastated with each second, fearing with every second that all was lost, it seems I recovered the bond with the world that had been cut loose in my master by the approach of death. I stopped waiting, even with humility, that comet's return in the gold dust from which we sometimes believe we descend. I don't want to be faithful to it, because it seems to reject waiting, fidelity and conquest through violence, even voluntary forgetting. A strange condition in which I struggle with great effort! But it's the world itself, it's danger that assists me—fighting against the confidence at the heart of which the fire that produced it dies, turning away constantly from purity, fidelity and hope, looking at its wounds, summoning me to immediate tasks, depriving me of what I love, castigating the beauty in which I would find a too-gentle death, it seems to want to push me deeper into a reality even more mysterious, more profound than the one I glimpsed and followed. However, I must stop in this path because if I draw the tracks, I know it will disappear again . . .

I briefly believed, like my master, that midway in my life's journey, still far from the peak, it was death I'd encountered—the bitterness, the horror, the lack of love, the renunciation of youth. Alone, I wandered through a city whose every monument seemed only another splendid and vain tomb. My joyous, my insolent defiance of despair was not able to resist certain blows of fate for long; perhaps age alone would have been enough to make me lower the tone. Now, I've changed. That something remains hidden from me, something in this world, in everything I see, do or undergo in following only common rules, that God remains silent, as is said, or is dead or definitively estranged, these two aspects in my opinion, far from depriving the world of its light, instead restore it. They are a kind of promise that promises nothing, a lamp one could not hope to carry, a call we cannot answer, at least not directly.

Perhaps it's the agile ones, the reckless ones who are right. I don't mean those who are sure of themselves, but those who accept and run the risk of losing themselves without hope of compensation. I don't at all consider myself one of them and I remained without affirming defeat or victory—for every affirmation is deceptive, because affirmation leads only into the obscurity of the age and if you use only affirmation for support, it will vanish as if it were nothing, like a breath that nonetheless cannot be confused with it.

I did not stop breathing—I constantly hear something breathing near me in the night. I can't say more about it. True love is a breath it seems nothing can interrupt.

Of my master, I know only that his ashes were scattered in a forest.